D1154756

Reaching Tin River

Also by Thea Astley

TWO BY ASTLEY
IT'S RAINING IN MANGO
BEACHMASTERS
AN ITEM FROM THE LATE NEWS
HUNTING THE WILD PINEAPPLE
A BOATLOAD OF HOME FOLK
THE SLOW NATIVES
THE WELL DRESSED EXPLORER
A DESCANT FOR GOSSIPS
GIRL WITH A MONKEY

REACHING TIN RIVER

Thea Astley

G. P. PUTNAM'S SONS
NEW YORK

G. P. Putnam's Sons
Publishers Since 1838
200 Madison Avenue
New York, NY 10016

Published simultaneously in Canada

Library of Congress Cataloging-in-Publication Data

Astley, Thea.
Reaching Tin River / Thea Astley.—1st American ed.
p. cm.
ISBN 0-399-13532-4
I. Title.
PR9619.3.A75R4 1990 89-38937 CIP
823—dc20

Printed in the United States of America
1 2 3 4 5 6 7 8 9 10

This book has been printed on acid-free paper.

"If this morning and this meeting are dreams, each of us has to believe that he is the dreamer. Perhaps we have stopped dreaming, perhaps not. Our obvious duty, meanwhile, is to accept the dream just as we accept the world and being born and seeing and breathing."

from "The Other" *(The Book of Sand)*
by Jorge Luis Borges
(translated by Norman Thomas di Giovanni)

I

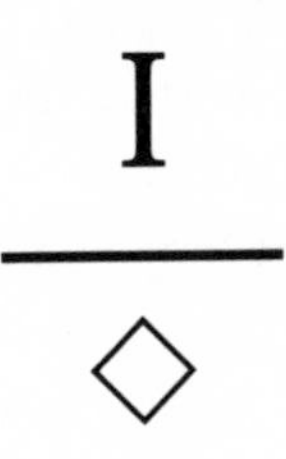

I am looking for a one-storey town
    with trees
    river
    hills
    and a population of under two thousand
    one of whom must be called Gaden Lockyer.

Or

    Mother was a drummer in her own all-women's group, a throbber of a lady with midlife zest and an off-center smile.

Or

    I have decided to make a list of all the convent girls who learnt to play "The Rustle of Spring" by Christian Sinding between 1945 and 1960.

I cannot invent reality. Time invents it for me. When I was at school I was always enraptured by the simple music of Euclidean geometry whose theorems and propositions disentangled themselves into solutions of total beauty. I argued with none of them except the definition on which theorems 27 and 28 of Euclid's Book I were based which stated that parallel lines on the same plane do not meet however far they are produced in either direction. Juxtaposing this statement alongside what my eyes perceived as I gazed down the railway track at Drenchings to a mystic coastal vanishing point I seem to have extracted an ultimate refutation. They met. Is the evidence of the eye always in opposition to that of the mind? I don't know the answer to this. I can write down only what I see—or what I think I see.

Or

> Oh mummy, mummy, I'll die, I'll simply die, if I have to leave Perjury Plains.

I must explain that Perjury Plains was the name of the family sheep property from which I was to be, age seven, untimely ripped (there's nothing like a little dalliance with Shakespeare to come chin up with the facts of life) and thrust into a coastal boarding school.

Or how about

> When I come back to the *bure* on the beach at Poindimié, I find Seb trying to hump the house girl. I say *trying*.

Or

> Tin River is a townlet of terminal attractiveness. Tin River is a state of mind.

Any of these might do for starters. Or even enders.

Each is true.

Each makes me what I am—the words, the eyescapes becoming fact not fiction. I can see that, peering through the streaked windscreen of three plus decades and knowing what I had missed most in life during my tender formation, for God's sake, was the after-school glass of milk and the cookie set out on a flowered plate on the kitchen table. I heard about it from the day girls at my school and when I stood in line with other boarders for the four-o'clock wedge of madeira cake or the thick slab of bread and butter, I dreamed of kitchens and mums and radios blaring behind that secure rattle of pots as dinner was prepared and the smells of roast lamb scented the air.

Where was mother?

Mother, I hesitated to tell my classmates (although I had confessed in cross-your-heart secrecy to Sheridan McAvoy, my plump best friend later to be known as Boobs), was unabashedly pounding drums in some school of arts or church hall while bush couples, their dedicated numbers shrinking, their bodies stiffening, plowed round the boraxed floor skidding through two-steps and fox-trots, jazz waltzes and barn dances. Old-time dancing had reached that point in its history where it was ready to be filmed and shoved in a time capsule for Martians to goggle at. But there they were, mother drumming, hands and breasts thudding, and Aunt Marie chopping away at a yellow-fanged upright, one foot pumping up and down, up and down on the sustaining pedal while she banged out "Jealousy" and "Deep Purple" and "Stardust." Hi there, Hoagy! Duke! Hi! Big beam from Aunt Marie to Bonnie on drums, Wilma on sax and then slip in a couple of tricky glissandos, the back of her right forefinger protected with a strip of sticking plaster.

There were always holidays, but not always mother.

Mother had grown up at Perjury Plains outside a lost townlet called Drenchings. She had a father, a mother and a sister, Marie, and although the sex of the children had been almost a terminal disappointment to grandfather who was looking forward to two cheap boundary riders, he resolved to make the best of it and bring them up tough. Small refinements, he assured grandmother, would be added at appropriate times. Bonnie and Marie could ride like stockmen before they were ten and take their turn at penning off and dagging by eleven.

"Is that really you, mum?" I would beg, pointing to the

snapshot of a pretty fair thing seated on a walloper of a stockhorse with a wild white eye. And it was. "Gee, you were pretty."

"Was I?" Even Mother looked baffled. "I never knew it, love. Pretty, eh? Then take a look at Marie."

Turning the pages of the old photograph albums, the family Debrett as it were, was the one thing that gave substance to my wavering, unsure center. I can relate my mother's past simply by the serial quality of those hundreds of fading snapshots.

"Look, there's Marie all togged up for the picnic races. She must have been sixteen then. How about her now? Yes, I can see what you mean, Belle darling. We *were* quite glamorous. Look at me, will you, all bows and frills. Quite ironic when your grandpa wanted boys. He didn't talk much, grandpa. As you know. Not to us. Except to give orders."

Grandfather, Bonnie told me, was always a loomingly silent man who only came to verbal life during biblical disasters like fire or flood or dusty exchanges at stock salesyards. I pleaded for family history. Bonnie doled it out in bits and pieces that I put together until the jigsaw, still with parts missing, covered my mind. When the girls reached puberty grandmother had packed away their correspondence school books and sent them off by train to a boarding school on the coast, a no-nonsense establishment tucked into the hills behind Brisbane. Four years later, their education interrupted, they would be brought back inland again, grandfather chair-bound on the homestead veranda with a stroke. *"Da capo,"* musical Bonnie had said, recalling their understudy years as stopgap drovers. The girls' early skills were put to ferocious use and their mother wept to see her pretty darlings who had sailed acne-free through adolescence grow weather-beaten before they had even investigated their youth. She complained to grandfather, tossing in words like "parties," "dances," "fun," phrases that went "having to work like men!"

Grandfather croaked from his spy-post, "Where's that equality you're always talking about?"

Grandmother ignored that and the year Marie turned eighteen threw a party. I can describe it as if I were there. It was one of my bedtime stories, the stuff of legend.

Imagine: It is mid-December. The homestead cracks in the heat. For hours after sunset the cooling roof will chatter mindlessly in the way I still remember. For six years there has been no rain and the dust spins up from arriving cars to sift its delicate beige arabesques into every room, coating the already drying bunches of eucalypt leaves grandmother has arranged artistically in jars. *Who came?* I pester mother on the edges of sleep. And mother, conscious of the drama of hiatus, pauses as she looks down on her only child and says, *Well let me see. Let me see.* She supposes over twenty, counting girls from town and neighboring properties, five older boys home from school for the holidays, three middle-aged shearers who had come in to Drenchings to spend their checks, a widowed lawyer from Jericho Flats and a bank clerk. She has omitted a vital piece of color. *With lots of teeth,* I squeal, *and flat feet.* Mother tucks this extra information in with the sheet curling round my face and I dream into that party. I reproduce that party for myself now.

The bank clerk was accompanied by a drum kit—snare, bass, hi-hat and ride cymbal. They were his entree, mother guessed, I guess, to more festivities than his flat feet and teeth deserved. When Bonnie or Marie took turns at the Bluthner, he would beat up the party with a semi-professional touch, making the ornaments in the room rattle responses to the floorboards bouncing under the feet of the dancers.

This story is told with pictures. Here's one of that very party, mother at piano under the sagging streamers, grinning at Cyril who has paused in his drumming to take a pull at a large jug of beer placed strategically on a side table. Even if mother had not told me she liked the drummer, I could have deduced that from the smile, the angle of her eye which is requesting something I am about to discover on turning the page or waiting for the next installment of my bedtime folktale. Yes, mother liked the drummer and she didn't mind that his feet were flat, finding the dazzling prominence of teeth gave him a boyish open look.

"Give me a turn," Bonnie demands, indicating the drums, the drumsticks.

Cyril is washing down asparagus rolls and little flecks of green cling to his teeth. *He thought I was joking,* Bonnie told me, *or crazy. A conservative boy,* she said. *He found the idea of a woman playing drums—well, gruesome.* Gruesome? *Like his awesome dentistry,* Bonnie said. She always had a flair for hyperbole.

I see them, I see them. He submits to such a pretty face, to such a smile. At the far end of the room grandmother is watching, dazed by the dangerousness of touching hair as the bank clerk instructs Bonnie on how to hold the sticks, how to control the beat. She sends Marie to intervene and Marie saunters to the piano and edges her sister away. *Lady drummer,* she giggles under her breath.

At this point my mother always inserts a drop of feminist philosophy. I can quote her verbatim to this day. "If there is something unladylike about hitting drums with sticks, then how would you describe dagging the backsides of sheep?"

Bonnie moves into Cyril's place. Marie sulks and begins

a jazz waltz. Bonnie ignores the crowd chaffing her, the irritated glares from grandfather, her mother's twittering. She plays. She plays the grins of the dancing guests and Cyril's toothy guffaws. She plays her sister's petulance and her parents' embarrassment and she has never been so pleased with herself. *Why?* I ask mother, sliding into slumber. *Why were you so pleased? I was a natural,* mother tells me. Dear mother. *Just a natural, Belle.*

Maybe, for moments, she was. But she never got any better.

There were not, Aunt Marie told me at other bedtimes, many parties at Perjury Plains. With grandfather pinned to a walking stick and unable to do much except in a roaring supervisory capacity, it fell to the three women to keep the place solvent. Grandfather was always reluctant to offer employment to outsiders when he could make full use of what lay to hand. By working from sunup to sundown, the three of them, aided only by casual labor, strained their way through two more seasons, and after dinner each evening would ask each other how long they could endure, antiphon for mother and girls, the chorus of which was supplied so endlessly by grandmother's lament that young women should be so trapped. Bonnie replied saucily after a particularly strenuous day, "I'm beginning to believe you."

"You really want to go, don't you?" grandmother asked fearfully.

"Of course we do," Bonnie said. Marie said.

One weekend they packed rebellious suitcases and were driven to the railhead by the bank clerk who proposed to each of them in turn as he saw an envied life-style vanishing from his life. Broad acres. Broad verandas. He seemed to have no concept of the realities of rural slavery. Mother and Aunt Marie fervently declined his offers of marriage but thanked him kindly and stood in the doorway of their carriage with buoyant tearless faces. There is a photo of this, too, taken by the bank clerk who smuggled the snapshot to grandmother a week after they had gone. They told him they didn't want to be farmers. Or farmers' wives, for that matter.

"But what will you do?" he asked.

They told him there would be something. There would always be something.

There was. They found office work in Brisbane within days and male admirers, as my mother coyly put it, within weeks. There was at that time a clutch of lonely American GIs on R and R leave from Korea. Bonnie was courted by a trumpet player from San Diego, a cheerful gumchewer who was within weeks of being drafted home, and trapped in Brisbane by clerical error. *Did you like him?* I would ask, as I was to ask myself years later. *Did you? Like him!* Bonnie was scoffing, *I was crazy about him.* The obvious depth of their mutual obsession and the Brisbane heat made Aunt Marie irritable and she foretold disaster. Once I discovered a photograph of the gumchewer grinning on a Gold Coast beach with a high surf behind him. *Your father,* Bonnie explained briefly and shoved the picture to the bottom of the pile from where, furtively, next day I pulled it out to examine my genetic history. He was a good-looking young man with a flopping forelock and the widest smile I had ever seen. I slipped the photo back where I could easily find it again and again. Why should this simple action have made me feel the first stabs of emerging conscience?

They marry.

Bonnie had recovered her authentic prettiness along with the air-conditioned change of occupation. Her only doubts were those flung at her by Marie. In the smoldering Brisbane weather, Huck *(I believe his name was Huckford,* mother says primly then bursts out laughing) pulls every compassion stop to speed the process before he departs. Grandfather wires from Drenchings, *Don't be a damned fool,* and the postmistress sniggers as she taps it out. Two days before Huck is due to fly out they are married. Grandmother just makes it to the coast and Marie, who had dispensed with her own gumchewer in one luminous row, is an unwilling bridesmaid.

I must insert some dialogue, filtered through family oral tradition.

"But what does he *do,* dear?" grandmother asks Bonnie later as they stand sobbing and waving through international airport glass.

"He's a trumpet player," Bonnie says between sobs.

"Yes, yes. I know that. But what does he do for a job?"

"That. He plays trumpet."

"I don't believe this," grandmother says. She checks with Marie to see if it is some horrible joke.

"Flugelhorn actually," Marie says, happy to add no comfort.

"Why don't you both come home?" their mother asks. "The place just isn't the same without you."

The plane is a vanishing speck. Bonnie's face is so wet with grief her makeup runs. Her eyes are tugged out, as it were, by vanishing love, and one arm still semaphores useless farewell. In the terrible heat the three women cling to each other and Marie whispers into her mother's ear, "You don't mean that. You know you don't mean that."

And grandmother whispers back, but loudly enough for them both to hear the blasphemy, "I hate the place too."

Waiting for the official permit that would allow her to join the almost stranger waiting for her across the water, Bonnie is nagged by misgiving despite the fact that the metaphor of what she had done in haste has a spurious attraction. The actuality, when she lies sleepless, barrages her with unknowns. She also flies out in tears.

Reunion with her trumpeter, now demobbed and living in a low-rent trailer park outside San Diego, is a matter of dubious bliss. After the first sexual frenzies wore themselves out in a matter of months, Bonnie found herself left alone a great deal as gigs took Huck up and down the west coast, sometimes as far away as Seattle. At first she used to travel with him and sit, an alien with an impossible accent, at a stage-side table prolonging her gin and lemon through set after set and finding her attention wander from the packed and smoky bars to the dried-out paddocks of home, the remembered insolent thumb of Mt. Zamia expressing what she was beginning to feel. She knew that the moment Huck lifted his instrument to his lips he forgot her. Maybe he would have trouble recalling her name.

I mention mother's pilgrimage in some detail to suggest a paradigm for my own. Her severance from the familiar must have had some turbulent effect upon what she was and what she became just as the fearsome cutoff delivered to me at age seven *(Mummy, mummy, I'll die if I have to leave Perjury Plains!)* when the boarding-school gates closed me off for terms like lifetimes from the things I knew and loved, bred in me a too-early self-sufficiency, a stifling of normal emotion, a tendency to hanker for the past.

Is this a meretricious explanation? I don't know. I can only write what I think it might be.

Right from the first, Bonnie told me once, she had begged Huck to have the band squeeze her in in some capacity.

Could she play piano now and again? They told her as kindly as they could that she wasn't good enough. *Drums?* she suggested. *How about drums?*

At this point mother would parody Huck's accent: *God, sugar, you want us laughed outa every joint?*

I admit, Bonnie said, *that I became a whimperer. I whimpered in public places while drinkers at nearby tables watched.* Huck began leaving her behind but as the whimpers persisted he was irritated into doing something and as a soother managed to bribe the drummer into promising her a few lessons. But when?

She hammered. She nagged. More parody: *For Chrissake, Bon!*

She won in the end. The band drummer got her seated just right and fixed up her hands much the same way as the flatfooted bank clerk had done in Drenchings and leant round her and demonstrated rolls and brushwork and fancy rhythms and said "You try, baby," and she did and her hands froze up.

Froze? I wonder.

I was nervous, Bonnie would tell me in a huffy self-justifying way. *Real nervous. I needed them to play along with me. I told them.*

"I need you to play," Bonnie said and all the band rolled long-suffering eyes at each other so she let her face screw up into subservient grief which walloped them. They all swung their instruments into position and the keyboards man started in on "Stars Fell on Alabama" despite Huck's loyal hisses that it was too hard while Bonnie's tears plopped on the snare drum. She laid down the sticks, and the drummer said, "Don't you worry, Bon. Don't you worry none. I'll give you lessons when we get back from L.A. and you'll be the best goddamn lady drummer on the west coast."

"She'll be the only goddamn lady drummer," Huck said bitterly.

But the band kept its jokes muted, even kindly, and when they came back from tour, Huck even bought his wife a secondhand drum kit he picked up cheap at a garage sale in La Jolla, and the sax player let her store it in a shed at the back of his house, so she could practice without driving the trailer park crazy, and for the next couple of months Bonnie went round there every few days and learnt to read charts and rap out basic rhythms.

"Mah pacifier," she told Huck, parodying again. "Ah need it."

And,

"I'm pregnant," she also told him at the commencement of her first American fall.

Perhaps this was my problem—being conceived in a trailer park ten thousand miles from what was ultimately to be my birthplace, my sensual landscape. If I were to draw up a balance sheet of personality profit and loss, that would have to go down in debit along with the idiosyncrasies of mother.

Am I merely looking for excuses?

Although Huck's response pretended jubilation (and here's another minus) Bonnie spotted the wry stretch of his usually smiling mouth that showed fractionally before he managed joy sounds. He barely earned enough money for two.

He hid his face against her in the warm middle of a hug. He joked that she should keep up that practice on drums. He said they would need every gig they could get. And he did a little finger-beat pattern on her stomach.

That was the first and only touch of my father's hand for thirty years.

On the band's next trip away up the coast, mother told

me (did I need to hear all this so young?) Huck stayed longer than he had needed, ringing Bonnie on the day he was due back with what sounded like a lie. Or a softened version of the facts. Bonnie took a cab over to the saxophone player's place and, finding no one there, began a muffled practice on the drums until someone in the house next door flung up a window and began shouting, "Stop that racket, lady! Please stop that goddamn racket!"

Instead of being offended, Bonnie was enraged. Spleen did wonders for her. She found herself a job in a roadside diner before her pregnancy began to show. The hours were so formidable, the shiftwork so frequent, she and Huck practically never met and when they did it was only to bicker. The relationship staggered on through vigorous morning sickness, through the baby's (my!) first uterine movements and, although Bonnie felt lost, unable to join the closed club of band talk, no longer welcome on their trips, she was saving most of her salary, the purpose behind her skinflinting unformed and lying at the back of her mind like a shadow fetus. She refused to give a name to it. Yet one evening, four months after she started the job and was just beginning a slight pregnancy waddle, everything came to a head.

"You're a godawful drummer, honey," Huck told her after listening to her tap away at "Georgia on My Mind." Not angrily, that was the terrible part; not even resentfully; just so matter-of-factly she was overwhelmed by the truth of it. "You'll never make a go of it."

The next weekend after she had seen the band off in their van, its blazoned sides, ROCKWARBLERS, obliterating itself in a blue haze of exhaust fumes, she packed her clothes, her trousseau underwear that no longer fitted, her photographs of Perjury Plains with her parents standing on the homestead veranda as the ultimate still-life, and rode a bus up the coast. She had just enough money for her plane fare back to Australia.

Where else but home?

"Feckless," her father told the runaway bride.

Bonnie had wept, strangely enough, at the sight of Drenchings' main street where nothing had changed. In the distance across the plains, Zamia's impudent rock thumb, purple-creviced in the cool lemon morning, displayed the same pattern-threat she had known all her life.

"This one might be a boy," her mother said.

II

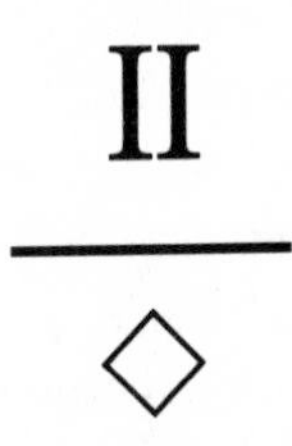

And another start.

I was born a month early on a late afternoon of the shearing season. So Bonnie tells me. Grandfather treated the whole business like a lambing. *With rather less concern,* she added. Mother was making a ten-pound fruitcake for the men and had bent to place it in the oven when the pains started. Perhaps it was the bending. Grandmother only just managed to intercept grandfather as he absentmindedly dialed the vet.

For months my wails dominated rooms, hallways, verandas. Time passed. I sat up. I crawled. I stood. I tottered forward lurching between chairs and cheers. I learned words. "Don't say that," grandma warned while Bonnie screeched with laughter. "That's an awful word." Singly. Then in pairs. "Don't say that either," grandma said. "It's awful! You're not to go near the sheds." Then whole groups of them while mother washed cleaned cooked. "I give up," grandma conceded. "She needs a nice school."

Aunt Marie returned home. The young salesman she had married soon after Bonnie flew to the States left for work one morning and rang later that night from somewhere in New Zealand. "I'm sorry, dear," he told her long-distance. "But I was so bored."

Wounded Aunt Marie played heartbreak numbers on the old Bluthner with lots of heavy pedal work and too much sway and eye-rolling as she worked out her damaged pride. It didn't take long. "I was bored too," she told Bonnie.

"Let's party, then," Bonnie suggested. "Let's celebrate celibacy! Let's go!" She bought another drum kit to replace the memory of Huck's gift and each weekend became a daze of bad music.

On Sunday afternoons as the sun tilted behind Mt. Zamia and even the flies were overcome by heat, the two young women had long soft talks on the veranda, plotting behind vermouth and ice. I could never interrupt enough.

"Not yet. You can see how it is." Bonnie jabbed her note of complaint along with a sandaled foot in my nagging direction. "She's still too young. I couldn't cope. She's too young."

I could not disentangle clues.

Words like *work* and *money* peppered these conversations and because I was aware of the threat of change, I raised my nuisance value to the nth power trying to impede conclusions. How did it happen that I could write down those words *Mother was a drummer in her own all-women's group?* How?

As my comprehension grew, their Greek chorus of complaint sorted itself out into long-remembered footnotes to the snapshots.

"I can't face," Aunt Marie said, "going back to that dreary office job in Brisbane, run by pimply oafs who can barely form a sentence but have all the competence in the world when it comes to pushing you around because you're the wrong sex. Overworked underpaid by air-brains. That damn pretentious store. Doing me a favor, I ask you!" (I realized later that Aunt Marie had teetered on the brink of unemployment largely because she was married.) " 'Taking jobs from men,' they said, 'in these hard economic times,' she would rant to Bonnie. 'My body requires food too,' I told them. 'You've a husband to support you,' they said. 'He spends all his money on beer,' I said. 'My goodness,' they said, 'what a way to talk and the honeymoon barely over!' 'What man,' I asked them, 'would want to spend his time cooped up all day behind a typewriter?' They said, 'We can give your job to some young girl who isn't lucky enough to have a husband.' 'Lucky!' I said. And I tipped my typewriter off my desk onto the section head's foot. 'Good heavens,' I said, 'I'm so sorry.' Then I cleaned out my desk and caught the first train back."

Tell me again, Aunt Marie, I would plead at bedtime. *Tell me how you lost your job.* And, *Here we go,* she would say, and I would join in at the climax, *Good heavens, I'm so sorry!*

Grandmother who overheard one night commented that it was improper moral training. We were too overcome with giggles to care.

How did it happen that I could write *My mother was a drummer in her own all-women's band?*

I must have been nearly four when mother and Aunt Marie made definitive moves by inserting advertisements into every bush newspaper for miles, tacked up notices on the doors of parish halls, rang friends on properties as far away as Allbut and Banana. The weekly music sessions had become daily practices. Grandfather threatened to leave. *What are you two up to?* grandma frequently asked. I was all ears. *What! You can't do this. Really. You'll give yourselves a reputation. As what?* they asked, interested. Curling up trying to be invisible on a lounge chair, I was interested too.

I don't know, grandma replied. *As something odd. Screwballs,* she ventured. *Is that the word?* (It became my word. I loved it. I said it over and over. What a talisman!)

Their musical twosome was a smash hit the first night they played for the Drenchings' Sheep Breeders' Convention. They extended their empire and played at the picnic races in Allbut and Banana. They were received with delight in Dingo and Jericho Flats. It must have been at this stage that the two of them decided to advertise in a Brisbane newspaper for a third member to plump out the musical tone of their act. Wilma was a former conservatorium student from Sydney who played clarinet. She also played saxophone and the whole of Drenchings fell about when she joined Bonnie and Marie for a New Year's shindig at the School of Arts hall. Wilma was too good for them but she added that professionalism they needed. Wilma on sax had the town clerk and councillors reeling. It was unwomanly. *Un-womb-man-ly,* Wilma explained later, punning in a way I wouldn't appreciate for years. *A lady on sax!*

It was 1964. I am six and a half. I lurk. I listen behind and in front of doors. I loiter near bedrooms. I shall write their dialogue with hindsight.

I see them now as I saw them one late afternoon when I ran to the empty woolshed where they practiced, to call them to tea. The air was granulated sun and dust.

"We need a name for the group. A name," Aunt Marie was insisting. "We can't," she said emphatically, "go on calling ourselves The Girls."

"Virgin Rock!" Bonnie suggested. She was staring out the woolshed door at the bleak landscape's one exaggerated feature. "God, doesn't it suit us!"

Marie said tartly, "And we don't play rock."

"We could try," Wilma said.

"What! Swivel and lurch? We'd be run out of town."

Wilma tapped the charts on the piano lid. "Don't say you weren't warned. Soon there'll be nothing else but." She began badgering the other two about improving attacks and cutoffs, the need for more inspired improvisation. "You've got the tempo. You've got the key. Play around with it for heaven's sake! Tease it a little."

Marie pulled a face. "I can't do it. I simply can't."

"Oh God, of course you can." Wilma snapped the hasps on her clarinet case. "All you do, Marie, is wham de wham de wham de wham. You could try. But you don't. You won't. It's no fun going whumpety whump all night. Who wants that?"

"They do," Marie argued. "The dancers want it. All those old boys and their partners togged up in their mothballed best. It's shiny satin time, sequin time, hair in the ol' tight perm time. We're not the star turn. We're subsidiary, can't you understand, to all those creaking joints having a great night out. They're making their own music."

Bonnie frowned. She said, "Marie's got a pretty good voice. We could jazz it up a bit by having her sing a number or two."

Wilma gave her a sharp look. "You serious? Okay, so the voice is big and the body too. But she ain't black. She ain't got it."

Marie went on as if no one had spoken. "They come to dance. Repeat, dance. Not to listen. You could play 'Three Blind Mice' and they wouldn't notice anything but the beat. If we start getting too fancy, they won't enjoy the dancing part, their bone music, and they won't damn well come."

"Nonsense!" Wilma began shuffling the sheet music, selecting, discarding, and then she slammed the lot down in an untidy skitter. "There's nothing wrong with making what we play more interesting musically, is there? More intelligent? I'm not asking you to intellectualize it for God's sake!''

She stomped out the door into sunset.

Wilma had been a student at the Sydney Conservatorium, the child of musicians who had banned all forms of profane music from the house. She, too, had been totally absorbed in the classical mysteries, until one weekend spent at a fellow student's flat, she heard an old Artie Shaw recording of ''Frenesi.'' ''It blew my mind,'' she told Marie and Bonnie. ''I simply didn't know that sort of stuff was going on.'' Conversion was blinding. Within days she had nosed out Buddy de Franco and Peewee Russell. She missed classes for a week as she sweated it out in her Balmain bed-sit trying to reproduce what she heard. She became obsessed (how well I understand that now). She combed record bars. When at last she returned from her explorations in new territory, her clarinet instructor asked icily what she had been doing. She smiled radiantly, picked up her instrument, blew a few starter notes and arpeggios, began a bird-like rendering of ''Der Hirt auf dem Felsen'' and then started to swing. Hello Schubert and goodbye! Wild improvisatory phrases ripped away from her breath and fingers and soared wildly and unrestrained through the open second floor windows of the building. The landscape began to liquefy in the summer rain of water and music.

''Stop!—Will you stop—that—at once!'' her teacher shouted, rushing to slam the window shut.

She was asked to leave. Her scholarship was withdrawn.

If she were a believer in signs, as I am, in the dissected innards of the chicken of convention, then this was it. She found it almost impossible, she told Bonnie and Marie, and incidentally the flapping ears of a small girl, to break into the world of jazz and pop music and knew that if she had stayed in her neat basic black and had been absorbed by an orchestra or chamber-music group, the playing of a wind instrument wouldn't have been unacceptable at all. There was a musical double standard and while it was preferred that she be playing violin or spreading her legs round a cello, it was possible for the concert-going intelligentsia (*Wankers!* Wilma cried bitterly) to accept women on brass and woodwind merely as an eccentricity. But out there in the clubs and pubs and bars, it would be a jokey matter, as unacceptable as a woman telling raunchy stories or propositioning a man. *Do you sing, love?* they asked Wilma. *No? Pity. We can handle women singers okay. Fact is, we like 'em. Bit of cling. Bit of tit and you're a sexy number, no sweat. But Jesus, love, you wanta get up there with the boys and mix it? No way! I don't think they'd like that. I don't think anyone would like that. My God, a sheila on clarinet!*

Knockback depleted her. Her response to Aunt Marie's advertisement was, we all knew, the end of the line.

At the last audition with a small-time group on the Gold Coast, she lost her temper.

"Just tell me why, goddamn you," she had demanded. "A good reason. Go on. Why?"

The bandleader had shuffled uncomfortably. He couldn't cope with female rage. Embarrassed, he directed a wink at the others.

"Look," Wilma screeched, intercepting the wink, "I'll tell you boneheads why. It's not that I'm no good. I'm damn good. I know I am. I don't even think it's a question of professional jealousy though there could be a bit of that. It's more basic than that even." Her voice had begun to crack with strain. As she relived the moment for Bonnie and Marie on the veranda at Drenchings, her voice cracked again. "It's a male preserve, isn't it? It's like women wanting the vote or drinking in public bars or trying to crash the members' stand at a poofter cricket match. You don't want to share the orgasm, do you? You're not ever going to say was it good for you too? God, you're pathetic. You bring your crummy little sexual attitudes into your public performance. The club. The fucking club."

I tell this as if I were there, fully mature and apprehending, but I can only say what I heard or think I heard. My mother and aunt had a way of rehashing old grievances and old stories until they gilded them as myth (whoever said *fucking* in those days?) and it was the myth that made my thoughts switchback on the bland grasslands of Perjury Plains.

I resolved, of course, never to play piano drums clarinet.

"You didn't have much talent, dear," mother would say to me later. "Not much musical ability at all. Strange how it can give one generation a miss."

I suppose I must have lisped the cliché "Where's daddy?"

Did I?

Oh you did. You certainly did.

Sometimes I even asked if we could have another daddy.

Mother explained inexplicably that she was still married. *Only legally of course. Daddy's over there,* she said.

Where?

America somewhere.

Actually she never bothered with divorce, and after the first jubilant bitterness of separation had settled into relief for them both, she and Huck exchanged cards now and then, small how-are-you letters and inexpensive parcels at Christmas and Thanksgiving. Mother sent photos of me. Huck replied with cuddly toys that I trailed round the sheepyards until they were too grubby for hugging. Neither ever mentioned the feasibility of reunion. Each preferred things as they were.

Bonnie's dance-group finally exhausted the possibilities of townships within driving range of Drenchings and my seven-year-old spy ears detected them working up to the necessity of a move. Bonnie pined for the coast. I was the difficulty.

As long as mother remained at Perjury Plains there was no problem with baby-sitters. My exhausted grandmother bore the brunt of me. Wilma, despite the fact that she had become almost a fixture in the household and could handle grandfather's attempts at bullying with an offhanded charm that stunned all of us, was becoming restless. The first I knew of a group decision to move east was the day they packed me into the van, bedding me down on a mattress among the instruments and suitcases, grandmother protesting through tears. They took two days to reach Townsville but after six months of lugging me along with them to sleep in change rooms at the back of dance halls, clubhouses and hotel bars, I became the youngest boarder at a small school outside Brisbane that seemed to specialize in the distraught progeny of divorce and government overseas postings. By the time I had learnt to make my own bed and stop crying myself to sleep at night, Wilma had left the group for Melbourne to become a variety act in a nightclub.

Bonnie and Marie were on their own again and who wanted their sort of music?

Who? Cow hicks? Yearning oldies? Maybe it was the sight of two still handsome but slowly middle-aging thumpers that made the dancers giggle more than was strictly necessary. Or appear to be giggling.

Grandmother paid my school fees and at term holidays and Christmas the little stranger was sent home to Perjury Plains so she could be measured, exclaimed over, checked for precocity and educational skills. They didn't know I was starting to regard the school as home.

I had stopped saying, *Mummy, mummy, I'll die if I have to leave Perjury Plains*. Long since.

One of my last stunning memories of the homestead is a broiler of a Christmas vacation and I, aged nine, playing shop with gibbers for groceries under the steps leading to our gracious veranda. Mother and Aunt Marie were away on the eventide circuit near Gladstone. Somewhere above me I could hear the sounds of teacups being refilled, the occasional comment of grandmother and grandfather's mumbled grudgers of replies when I suddenly chucked down the handful of gumleaves and pebbles that represented currency and sobbed. I sobbed as if I wanted to dissolve within my own salty tears. "I want love," I heard myself whispering. I'm not sure what I meant. I can only say what I said, or thought I said. But those few whispered words brought into opposition a maturity and innocence that understood nothing at all except a yawning emptiness and boredom. Not even later, when I heard other students talking about boys or tried not to hear two of the prefects canoodling in the dormitory bed opposite mine, would I be able to interpret the emptiness of that moment.

I stalked round to the front of the veranda steps and trod up them with a lumpish deliberation to announce challengingly to grandma that I would never play piano. Never.

Grandma handed me a chocolate biscuit hoping it would soothe.

She understood, more that I did, the reason behind the words.

"We'll see, dear. We'll see. Eat up your biscuit. There are worse things than having to learn piano." She gave an odd and tiny smile.

"What?"

I looked across at grandfather but he appeared to have gone to sleep except for the glisten of eyeball I detected between his narrowed lids.

"Lots, darling. Lots. You'll discover. It's an escape hatch, believe me."

The opening argument for the defense!

By my twelfth birthday Bonnie and Marie, welded into a partnership stronger than marriage, a kind of twinhood sanctified and integrated by cornball rhythms and sugar-candy tunes, had got their feet in the doors of several down-market Brisbane clubs and had settled into a dedicated impoverishment at a bayside suburb, living in a set of furnished rooms in a boardinghouse near Shorncliffe, a ramshackle timber scramble called Villa Marina.

They were to be there for the next seven years.

"It's handy, darling." Mother always believed in exploring expediency. "Your school's just across the bay. We could almost wave to each other. You can come home each weekend."

"Home?"

"Here."

"It's hideous. How can I tell the other kids I live in this dump? How can I ever ask them here?"

"It's not hideous, Belle. It's homely and friendly and it saves Marie and me from housework. Well, more or less. And it gives us freedom for daytime jobs."

Economics had forced submission. They were now both

working as checkout assistants in a local supermarket. Engagements were becoming fewer as the electronic age forced musicians to the wall. And especially their sort of musician. Dance engagements, even in outer suburbs or the less savory parts of South Brisbane and Fortitude Valley, dwindled to a trickle, for who wanted, in this post-Beatle era, the sort of sounds that would engage the attention of graybeards only, pensioner groupies wanting to wallow in nostalgia. Even their sort of dancing was gone. People stood in front of other people and shook like holy rollers. Body contact was being kept for muggers.

Bonnie and Marie lied bravely to me to explain the checkout jobs. "Icing on the cake," they said. "Icing."

Yet inexorably, steadily, I was becoming interested in the ramifications of nostalgia.

Mother was thirty-three, -four. She looked more. Her figure had thickened and became magisterial. She wore her beautiful gold hair hacked into a cropped cap that was easy to deal with. She wore sensible shoes. Every afternoon after work mother and Aunt Marie would enter phase one of their health kick, don bathers and swim in the limpid bay waters from beach to pier-end and back half a dozen times. Both of them developed shoulders like policemen's. Their skin had a pickled look from saltwater. But they gave off the boisterous confidence of men-free women who, having achieved and now eschewed matrimony, managed to support themselves. Mother had long since ceased writing to Huck or accepting checks from grandfather's sheep.

I should have been proud of her, of them, of this conquering of the economic slave system so geared against females but on school sports days or prize-givings, at fetes and breakup concerts, I would cringe as mother and aunt appeared like twin constables *(The praetors!* one of my nastier friends would whisper), ready for a bit of girls-together reminiscence and cheeroh. As they wandered through the school grounds under the camphor laurels and the fig trees, I would try to lose them, pretend they were some anonymous part of the crowd of parents and guardians who were sauntering across the lawns. My classmates, however, always directed my attention to them. *Hey hey hey! There's Bonnie and Clyde!* Choruses of sniggers. I wanted to die.

"We want the best for you," Bonnie had often told me. As grandma had. "Only the best. You must do well, Belle dear, for there's nothing like a good education." (Was this really mother speaking? The original screwball from Drenchings?)

"Not even the piano?" I would reply unpleasantly, for I was then and had been for some years, an unwilling learner.

"I will forget," Bonnie said icily, "that I heard that."

Another year. And another. I am fifteen.

I shall put my personality cards on the table.

I am staying at Villa Marina for the August holidays; Mother and Aunt Marie are on their annual leave from the checkout counters and are doing one- and two-night stands in the Mary Valley.

There are four permanents in this downmarket Rattigan boardinghouse on the bayfront, but the two who matter to me are not there to give comfort.

Hello Mrs. Burgoyne of the still pretty elderly face and the soft overrefined vowels she employs in her teaching capacity at the local grade school and the mouth like dry paper until it is touched up with a rose-pink lipstick, the merest stroke, especially on school inspection days. "You'll know when it's inspection time," Bonnie has told me. "She'll douse herself in Nuits de Curriculum."

So doused.

I imagine her as sixty, seventy, one hundred and seventy, but she must have been in her late fifties I understand now counting on my worn adult abacus. I am frightened of her age and her unrelieved refinement, of her crankiness and her ability to see through.

"You'll like Mr. Renouf," she had said to me as we walk in together to dinner. Her smile is too astute.

And *Hello Mr. Renouf.*

Mr. Renouf is the wreckage of a handsome man, a towering still elegant leaf-weight widower with an interested elderly eye. In previous years he was usually to be found roosted on a deck chair on Villa Marina's front veranda while I raced past in my bathers to swim with mother and aunt in the tepid bay water. "Good swim?" he would ask indifferently. He is a retired merchant navy man and the telescope to his eye, I realized at twelve, scanned only horizons. "Cold in?" That rheumy blue would be nowhere near me but Mrs. Burgoyne would always smile at me, past and through and up the stairs to my narrow bedroom. Eight by ten by twelve. The twelve's the height. One window and a holland blind, a stretcher, a clothes cupboard, a dressing table drunk with seventy years of salt air. Shorncliffe is an old village in an arm of the bay where the sea crawls in to jetties and mudflats and mangroves. In the park, the hardly patronized fish cafe stands high, with glass walls gaping at the sea, reflecting yachts and fishing boats prowling the sea-lanes.

At night darkness clumps from the air, falls over and through the Moreton Bay figs like black syrup.

"Meh husband, Tesman . . ." Mrs. Burgoyne would often say, mumble mumble.

(He was dead? She was separated? Why didn't I listen more carefully?) I know she's a lonely widow of uncertain temper teaching beautiful copperplate and complicated money additions to ungrateful nine-year-olds. Later, when I was also teaching at the same grade school, I observed how the men on the staff brought out her terrible flirtatiousness but it was me they were kind to. Fatherly. The kid. Be nice to the kid. *Where's mother? Banging drums in a disco, Mr. Bonsey.*

Why am I in this dump?

Why am I in this dingy dining room where we dip for soup in broken rhythm and fork up dubious roast and veg?

I go to breakfast, lunch, dinner and try not to talk to anyone. Mrs. Burgoyne tells me it is rude to read at the table. I know it's rude and it is my protection. Yet I close the offending book quickly, being still responsive to the reproof of elders and smile my apologies. Some residue of powder is trapped in the soft creases of skin about her mouth, and her lipstick has coursed little rivers into the downturns at each corner although she is harrowingly widow-smart.

I am cruel. I am young.

She nods approvingly at my obedience, graciously acknowledging so that I feel I have been given papal absolution. She tells Mr. Renouf that it is a lovely afternoon and I watch slyly for his response for now Mr. Renouf has been watching me and Mrs. Burgoyne's preludes flutter around and away like broken butterflies.

''No, May,'' Mr. Renouf complains to the maid. ''I said no beans.''

''Meh soup, dear,'' Mrs. Burgoyne reminds. ''You've forgotten meh soup.''

''It's off now, Mrs. B. You was late.''

''Eh em never late.''

There will be five weeks of this.

Mr. Renouf is watching me again, a tiny smile (why? why?) on his age-freckled face. I decide to give him something to smile about, to widen that skin-stretch on his boulevardier visage. After lunch I go upstairs to my room and change into my new swimsuit. It is black and rather daringly cut. My own fairness is outrageous. *Almost albino,* Marie says unkindly when I annoy her. *Like a negative, aren't you, darling?*

I stand absorbing myself in the wardrobe mirror, a spotted sliver of glass attached to the inside of one of the wardrobe doors. I slip on sandals with unsensible heels and sling a psychedelic beach-towel over one shoulder. I absorb again. I remember Aunt Marie's remark and watch my face react with resentment. It's true. I am almost a negative. But other words rock through me. Young young young. I refuse to admit anything else. Nothing else. Does anything else matter? The face is—reasonable, perhaps pretty at certain angles or in certain moods; the body is a slim and developing ghost. I blow myself an ironic kiss. *Ooooh Mr. Renouf,* I simper, and close the wardrobe door on the mirror. My reflection remains in the mirror and smiles at the empty space.

Already Mr. Renouf is seated for his post-luncheon pipe, fuzzily gazing through the giant figs of the park at lost blue roadways. He's in one of those deck chairs with wide extendable arms on which legs or drinks may be propped. Where is the drink? Where are the lazy feet? There is no sign of decadence except that aromatic pipe. His bony knees could almost slash back at the knife-creases in his dated gray flannel casuals.

Too slowly I saunter past his chair, too close, and pause at the top of the steps where the sun gropes for me like a lover until I turn my back on it and my own smile into Mr. Renouf's.

He nods. He smiles and nods. Is it approval? Can those rheumy eyes really see me. He says, "Lovely day for it."

For what?

Mrs. Burgoyne is a pink and gray manifestation of perfume in the hall doorway watching us both.

"You'll get horribly sunburnt, dear, in that—that costume," she says hopefully. "You should take more care of your skin."

I drop my towel on her remark, exposing more, and wave a languid fringe of fingers, provoking her. There is a lot more skin as I dangle the towel on the veranda floorboards.

When I come back from the beach through the little park, I can see Mr. Renouf still sitting on the veranda. My hair is flattened, my body stinging with salt. My bathers cling like a second skin but now I feel more the small girl, wanting to gambol on the thick turf, be applauded and laughed at and approved. *Good girl,* I long to hear someone say. (Where is mother?) *That's the girl. Good girl. You're back then. You took care. Was it lovely in?* Where is mother? Anyone?

Mother is beating drums in every country dance-hall north and south of Kin Kin. I bet she's copping a lot of slow claps, hoots. There's irony for you.

Mrs. Burgoyne and Mr. Renouf are posed on the stoop like a couple at Bournemouth boardinghouse. Any minute the band will start its tarum-ta-ta on the pier. But it's different here. There's a touch of Diane Arbus. There's sun and almost white sand and a racing blue sky under which the whole of Brisbane bakes its prejudices. The two of them watch me drip across the road, through the gate, along the garden path to the foot of the steps.

I flaunt myself. See me, Mr. Renouf! See me in my half-naked state, costume gripping. Want me? Someone want me. And Mrs. Burgoyne says, her paper-strip lips looking like Band-Aids, "Why, Belle dear, you're very red. Very. Does it hurt?"

I catch Mr. Renouf's aged eye traveling a scarcely remembered journey up my legs which are now become his abstraction, a half smile still on his mouth, and I say,

"Everything hurts, Mrs. Burgoyne."

That week is full of silent turmoil.

Beneath the silence can be detected the violence of resentments and jealousy, of screaming domestic rows conducted pianissimo. May, the dining-room maid, is married to a local busdriver, a wiry and intense mustachioed masher whom I see chatting up a sunny redhead no older than I am every time I catch the bus to the railway station. They huddle when she buys her ticket with the intimacy of lovers. In the cold way of adolescence, I understand. May is twig-thin from running her gaunt body between kitchen and tables, from washing up and sweeping floors. Already she is lined like a fifty-year-old. Her eyes are gummy from tears. One appears to have been blackened. As she wilts, husband Reg blooms. Mrs. Burgoyne has had a verbal tiff with Mr. Renouf. She cuts him dead at breakfast and lunch but relents towards dinnertime. I wonder about alternatives to the burden of marriage.

After dinner these evenings I sit a little longer in the shared sitting-room across the hall from the dining room. There are salt-riddled lace curtains, six easy chairs of yellow vinyl and a black-and-white television set whose images waver and wobble so excessively it is hardly worth turning on. There is also an old piano. On the coffee table are piled five-year-old copies of *Newsweek, Time* and *Woman's Day.* It could be a dentist's waiting room.

I am waiting for a tooth to be pulled.

I extract a thought.

I shall make a list of all the convent-school girls who learned to play "The Rustle of Spring" by Christian Sinding (born 11/1/1856, died 3/12/1941), between the years 1945 and 1960. It will be a prodigious project.

It would be an enormous task for anyone normal but already I sense I am not quite that. I have developed a penchant for lists and for the camera. *(Stand still, mother! Just for a minute, will you! Marie, make mother stand still! It's my only chance of getting to know her.)* Photographs give me a reality to clutch at—or a sense of it. And my bulky snapshot albums accept this new project as respite.

I'd bet my bottom dollar Mrs. Burgoyne played "The Rustle of Spring" in her heyday. *Oh Mrs. Burgoyne,* I shall ask at breakfast next morning, *did you ever play "The Rustle of Spring"?*

And Mrs. Burgoyne will take a tiny handkerchief of spotted muslin and dab tea-wet from her upper lip and the little dribbles at each corner of her mouth and her eyes will be suddenly sharp.

Oh I did, she will say. *Why do you ask?*

I shall make wordless sounds.

"It wasn't meh party piece," she confides in actuality a few days later to my concealed and rude teenage mirth, "not really. Not that. I used to play Ketèlbey, dear, whenever I was asked. "Bells Across the Meadows." I'm sure you've never heard of him. A lovely rippling piece. And there was another. Let me see." Mumble mumble.

" 'In a Monastery Garden,' " I say confidently, spoiling the whole conversation for her.

She glares into my cocky eyes.

"Yes. Why yes. How on earth did you know?"

Mr. Renouf is observing Mrs. Burgoyne shake with annoyance as she reaches for the butter and begins scraping the last of it across cold toast.

"I'm sure you could still play it!" he says gallantly, the silly old bugger. Why suggest it even?

There is a great deal of agitated movement on her chair at this, simpering and wafts of eau de cologne.

"Tonight," she half-promises. "Perhaps tonight."

There she would be, I imagined, cushioned with excuses—*I'm dreadfully out of, the piano hasn't been tuned in, cannot remember after*—swaying her top-heavy but frail torso at the out-of-tune Challen in our private parlor, her bum looking wider on the piano stool than it should, her arms busy under see-through voile, all feminine allure while the wrong notes jangle.

I was cruel. I was wrong. She played like a professional. I would applaud till I had to be removed.

I begin my list.

"A school project," I explain to returned Bonnie and Marie, to the library assistants at Sandgate, to Mrs. Rose Burgoyne and Mr. Clarrie Renouf. I do not reveal its nature. Boredom, the long stretch of vacation, even Bonnie's reminiscences, inspire my mania.

Play something, dear, they had always asked grandmother and then Bonnie and Marie (they never now asked me, being electronically sated) in those corseted sweating country evenings. "It was like a nightmare," Bonnie sighed. In every Saturday-night living room, the piano threatened Liszt consolations, Chopin preludes and Brahms rhapsodies, rattled off prestissimo. And like a nimbus, "The Rustle of Spring." Spring has never rustled in that part of the country, but nevertheless spruced-up husbands endured spring as they champed on pipes, sucked cigarettes or tried to hide themselves on shadowy verandas. Scabby-kneed kids lingered, picking at shins in doorways. The hostess always had three sorts of sponge and a boiled fruitcake. Cracker biscuits were topped with mounds of cheese and tomato savory.

"Do play something dear."

"Play?"

"Yes dear. Something pretty."

"Pretty?"

"Well, you know."

"Bash 'em some Bach," Marie used to whisper to Bonnie.

"No no, dear. Not that. That's too—intellectual. Something . . ."

" 'Rustle of Spring?' "

"Oh yes, dear. That would be lovely."

"It was nearly always 'The Rustle of Spring.' "

"Nearly?"

"Always. Always always always."

"Shit," Marie would hiss behind a cracker. "That Sin—ding!"

Sometimes one of them would whack through the "Raindrop Prelude" or dazzle with the "Minute Waltz" (I think Chopin really meant min*ute!)* played in fifty-five seconds flat, but one starter movement only of a Beethoven sonata had the guests writhing while outside the interpreted white moon scalded the inland plains and slapped wash-silver down the sides of the virgin rock.

"No dear. I didn't mean that piece. I meant that other piece. You know . . ."

"Ah! 'The Rustle of Spring!' "

"Lovely, dear," they always said when the last whining motif was hacked through. "Really lovely!" What a lovely touch she has—Ena, Gert, Maureen, Bonnie. What a lovely touch!

The vision of old Fred Bathgate, my teacher and mother's, intrudes at this point to be flashed cholerically into all those spring-rustled living rooms, convent practice studios, school concert halls.

Oh—my—God!

So, I am making my list.

Already I have two thousand eight hundred and forty-five names—and that's only Brisbane. It hasn't been easy making this list, mark you. I started off with all the girls I knew who had learnt it and reached one hundred and seven in under an hour. Maybe it would have been easier to make a list of all the girls who didn't learn to play it. I'm one of those. One of the lucky few.

Aunt Marie reinforces Bonnie's stories.

"I guess it was a nightmare," Marie agreed. "There was always some splendid girl in white who'd seat herself, no sweat, at the piano and off she would sail. We never had spring, for God's sake, and I was only ten and for a while I didn't think there were any other pieces. Maybe Mozart's 'Rondo alla Turca' or that goddam 'Raindrop Prelude.' God! 'The Raindrop Prelude!' And the sheep were all keeling over in dozens in the muddied water-holes and claypans."

"Oooh," Bonnie interrupted, her eyes glistening, "I

heard de Falla once, 'The Ritual Fire Dance,' at one of Mr. Bathgate's student concerts. I don't think they taught that either at the convent. I think the nuns would have thought it too inflammatory. Every Saturday, Belle, Marie and I were allowed to go to dear old Fred's studio, just like you. What a pet! Anyway, we learnt masses of Bach and Mozart and Haydn and lots of Clementi studies. Especially those. So you can imagine how 'Rustle' affected me when I heard it for the first time ripped out by the head girl in one of the practice rooms. All those trills and bird tweetings and leaf shakings. The convent was pretty big on Grainger's 'Country Gardens,' too, and a terrible thing called 'Bells Across the Meadows.' You notice, Belle, how all those pieces were gentle nature scenes, tralala, English, non-Australian in flavor and with pastoral evocations unlikely to arouse our girlish senses. This is sex instruction, darling."

"We didn't have any girlish senses," Marie put in at that point. "I think they still remembered the horrors of the American invasion."

I, Belle, never hear "Rustle" or "Bells" these days. Yet one morning just before or just after Mrs. Burgoyne's recital, I can't remember exactly, I heard an announcer on national radio say, "The next piece will be a no-frills version of 'The Rustle of Spring.' "

How do you like that, Christian? Does it stun you up there in Oslo, composer of "The Holy Mountain," three symphonies and the "Rondo Infinito!" Pretty rude, eh? I couldn't believe it. Anyway, this version sounded much the same to me, the same that grandmother, when nagged, could dish out at seventy, her fingers moving automatically into all the right places on the keyboard. The same that all my piano-playing classmates could whip through. What was this no-frills business? I couldn't believe it. Glued to the radio. No frills? There was the same family-and-friend-sized package. There were the same whistlings and whooflings, shakings and tremblings that used to be served out or dished up, as Bonnie relates, to the accompaniment of all those supper sponges.

That really started it. The list, I mean. So back to that for a minute as I give my no-frills version of the growth of obsession.

I drew up a pro forma letter.

It was difficult to word my inquiry without sounding unhinged.

I spent a lot of time at the bayside library where the smell of old books and newspapers besotted me. I used their photocopier until it caused comment. I posted those letters off in their dozens to every convent in the state (did I miss a couple?) with a postscript plea to pass on my request to any older or retired music teachers.

Why do this? Was it the boredom of my Brisbane evenings? Brisbane was/is a very boring town on its interrogatory river miles from the sea with its grilling summers, its undramatic winters.

Largely, my inquiries were ignored, not literally perhaps, because nuns are very polite. But they passed over the nub of my letter with evasively courteous replies . . . *we have read your letter with interest* (read amusement) *but feel the answer to your problem* (I had presented myself as a thesis hunter) *is out of our range. We suggest you apply to the Australian Music Examinations Board or the Trinity College of London who might be able to give you a list of the years that particular piece* (I want to spell it ''peece'') *was on the syllabus. We believe Trinity College made use of it a number of times as did the AMEB. Perhaps their examiners could help you.*

Then they asked God to bless me and remained mine sincerely.

Talk about passing the buck! And I thought they were dedicated, especially to the mania of detail.

I am discovering the limits of dedication, particularly that of others. Am I thinking here of my mother's tensed interests which seem to make me peripheral? I am certainly discovering, this hot and boring summer, the non-limits of my own, which seem infinite or inexhaustible or perhaps unattainable.

I am dedicated. I have the capacity. Well, that's how I see it.

There was one letter that delighted me:

I estimate, the trendy nun wrote in impeccable cursive, *that over thirty years (I am now retired from active teaching, thank God) I taught that particular work to six hundred students. I cannot possibly recall their names but have based my figures on note-books and order-lists I still have with me. Every one of them played it technically well—I saw to that—and with emotional indifference to which I contributed no emphasis at all.*

She didn't ask God to bless me but was mine amusedly, Sister Mary Perpetua.

There was a postscript:

Your inquiry strikes me, may God forgive me, as idiotic. I hope I never have to hear "The Rustle of Spring" again. At my age that is a joyous possibility.

Hi, Sister Perpetua! Salud!

So I now have two thousand eight hundred and forty-five players, almost all nameless, when I total those schools kind enough to hazard a figure, plus another six hundred and forty-nine that I shall simply list as Perpetua 1, Perpetua 2, etc.

Is there any point in this?

Maybe not, but the exercise has served to whet my appetite for the desired exactness of research, of its contingent excitements, and it has made me, too, want to investigate the psyche of dear Fred Bathgate who, Bonnie and Marie swear, in the five or six years in which they maddened each other, never once made reference to "The Rustle of Spring" and whom, Bonnie insists, although he was long since dead, she once saw waiting near the Grey Street bypass at a particularly busy point where the traffic swings over the river to the new concert center. What was he doing there? Was he about to fling himself beneath the traffic because someone had forced him to *listen* to "The Rustle of Spring?" He must have been an outstanding man, Bonnie says mournfully, never to have uttered those four words.

He was certainly long-suffering.

"You come here to do your practice," he reprimanded me during those four years of our own relationship as I sight-read my Czerny for the week—with cachet, I insist. I was a good sight reader and hoped to delude him. I used to practice other distracting measures by illustrating the title pages of my sheet music with mood sketches intended to capture the evocations of the notes. "They look," he commented coldly once on a texta set of Tchaikovsky mountain peaks and coming up behind me as I played to crush correcting arms about my own, "like ill-fitting dentures." Then he took over himself, his ginger-haired paws racing up and down the keyboard. "Like *this!*" he said, squeezing to emphasize. "And *this*. Or *this*" Relaxing his pinioning arms. "Now try again."

Yes. He taught me as well. Mother won that round and I have to admit that his personality, the escape from school routine each Saturday morning and, yes, the music itself, gave me glimpses of a notable centrality. *If two circles touch one another,* says theorem 48, *the centers and the point of contact are in one straight line.* Mr. Bathgate, could you have been my center?

There was no question of doing my licentiate. All the girls, mother told me, who played "The Rustle of Spring," did their licentiate. They dated events from that moment.

"Do you want to play," Mr. Bathgate would ask me, "or do you want to pass exams?"

"Play," I would whisper.

"Then for God's sake practice! And not here. Now do that again."

And he would stalk away from me in his baggy tweeds and slump, suffering, in an easy chair across the room, or bound back suddenly exasperated, edging me nearly off the piano seat as he demonstrated my musical incomprehension. Mr. Bathgate, indeed you were my center, if only for those brief hours when I strove to implement what you taught.

"No no no!" He would play the whole work through, easily, sensibly, movingly. My soul would blush.

No licentiate. Maybe my lack of qualification has made me what I am. Once at the most boring slides evening *(That's me at Yellowstone! Look! There I am on the beach at Oahu! See! What a scream!)* I have ever unwillingly attended, a chubby matron pal of Bonnie's asked her husband about a pre-nuptial shot: *Daddy, when was that taken? Wasn't it the year just after I got my letters?*

Was it dear? he replied. And he had looked slyly sideways at me and winked with the eye away from her.

There were girls at my school who practiced till their fingers throbbed before taking out their licentiate but they never played a note afterwards. The qualification, not the music, was their center. Funny. Bonnie was rather like that. She learned "The Rustle of Spring" on the sly and took up drums. There's no accounting.

"No wonder," old Mr. Bathgate said to me as we talked on the front porch of his New Farm house, lesson over, watching the silver-mud glint of the river and the color blobs of the roses in the park across the road. He refused to repeat the title. I felt treacherous towards Bonnie. As I slipped the cup of tea he always gave me after lessons, I watched him clench and unclench his fingers as he muttered to himself. I hoped he was only exercising his hands.

After I turned fifteen my piano lessons came to an end. Mr. Bathgate had died while holidaying with friends down the coast. His death ached in me like a tooth. For the rest of the school year I missed him, longing for those sparring Saturday mornings when he made reproofs and told me to practice at my own place. Just to know him had done something: I kept on with my practice and bought the sort of music I thought he might like me to learn, and I thought of him often.

Bonnie and Marie had wept for him too and dragged me (unwilling to confront a death) to the funeral where the three of us, aunt, mother, child, stood in a forlorn group at the cemetery and cried for our lost youth as much as for Fred.

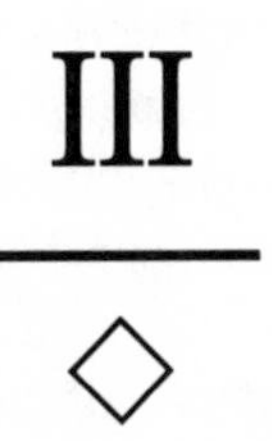

Three years later I am returned to Villa Marina, student teaching at the beach school, Mrs. Burgoyne about to receive an ovenware farewell, Mr. Renouf removed to a twilight home farther round the bay known as "God's Waiting Room," and Bonnie and Marie still rubbing out an existence from their small apartment at the rear of the boardinghouse. I insist on my own room upstairs. I am supposed to be adult. I have never been a child. For one who has been an adult for nearly twenty years I have an idiotic innocence.

Back late from Brisbane one cultural evening of live theater, walking from the railway station into the treed blackness of the uphill road, hurrying and trying not to hurry, I am almost frightened to death by Wazza, the yardman, from Villa Marina, padding up behind me in the dark and growling pleasantly, "I'll walk you home, Belle." Wazza is a kindly giant with a tinplate in his skull, a present from Vietnam. *He's a bit—well—thick,* they all said.

"Here we go," Wazza says.

Indeed.

The front steps of Villa Marina are sand-white in moon and seashine but the rest of the place is strangely dark. I assume skinflint management or a general fuse. Upstairs the corridor light-switch wobbles uselessly and I feel my way, blinded, a foot at a time, along the people-pens, groping, miscounting doors and opening what I think is mine on a blazing cube of pornographic posters, a peak-hour density of breasts, thighs, pudenda; and swinging on me with a snarl from the bed-edge where it is haunched, a skeleton. Not a skeleton, I observe in the half-gasp all this horror takes. There is evidence of papery flesh, sparse gray thatch, the blaze of a gas lamp. Who is he? When had he come to thrust his miserable solitariness into the house? Never seen at meals. His gauntness humps there on his stretcher-bed below the flaring sumptuousness of the walls. The horror of it! The terrible whiteness! Groined in, his agony of a face is cracking into a yawp. I have a flashing vision of myself five years before flaunting myself on the lawn steps and

"Sorry," I manage. "Oh my God, sorry!" as he begins to heave himself up even as I back, back wildly, slamming the door on this tiny hell, clawing my frenzied way out in the dark, to hear Wazza calling from the hall below, "You okay there?"

In. Through.

My narrow single bed. The blessed bareness of my own cell. The book on the dressing table still open at the page I had last reached, the ordinary saneness of it, and the light, thank God, working for only a moment before it flutters out. I shudder into bed to swelter sleepless in summer fug, mosquitoes droning in from the opened window, the mosquito net suffocating, a chair rammed under my door handle.

What is the reason for my outrage, my terror? The old man's frailty snuffed out any notion of physical threat. I am not a prude yet I am disgusted by his needs. I have read a lot about sex and I am still a virgin. I am assaulted by the realization that my gender is meat.

Days later as I sit observing the dust filter its brown

flowers into that sun-hard room, student friends from town knock on my door to commiserate, to see, to . . . "Talk," I order them. "Talk talk talk. Please. I'm going crazy for lack of talk." (Bonnie and Marie are swanning around a Barrier Reef island on annual leave from the checkout.)

We wander into afternoon along the cliff road above that shifting bay crescented with mud flats in an ebb tide. We talk. We watch night settle onto the water and the lights come out along the shoreline. And we talk. We find the fish café open beyond the trees in the park and the moon comes up above the sea and watches us watching it.

"You can't stay there," my friends advise, almost elderly in their concern. "You can't. It's unspeakable. It sounds like a squat for loonies. It's not amusing seedy. It's the pits."

"Mother," I say. "Mother's there. Well, not at the moment. But mostly. She's there as it were. A presence."

"But how can she bear it either?"

"She's eccentric."

I swallow resentment that tastes of fish and lemon.

As we sit, the moon burns out from orange to ash, floating through its own illusion of freedom. Like me, I think. Moon Belle. I am urged to give up teaching, to get a job in the city, to find work that doesn't dehumanize. My friends analyze my situation with ruthless tongues. Their pejoratives spare nothing. *The scumline,* they say. *What is? Your job. Your living situation.* Well, what can one do with an eight-by-twelve cell, a puritanically narrow bed, one door, one window, even the old man (whom I am beginning to understand through my repulsion) in the next room? What can one do with a communal bathroom, a waterlogged downstairs laundry? Years later, baking on the coral sand at Poindimié before another epiphany, I ask myself if I had ever used that bathroom, that slum of a laundry. I must have. And I marvel at the mind's ability to obliterate the distasteful.

With respect, they tell me, *your mother's a nut. No offense.*

"That's what I like," I say loyally. "I couldn't bear it if she wasn't."

Forward slouch! Mr. Bonsey, committed socialist and teacher of grade six, shouts whimsically to the morning assembly.

I am the only one to choke on giggles. Mr. Bonsey who is small and neat and faintly Lebanese-looking flashes me a smile of appreciation without really catching my eye and I see Mrs. Burgoyne along the line of staff (it is her last day but one) make a critical bud of her mouth. *Rose thou art sick.*

"I have been meaning," Mr. Bonsey says to me as we stalk the schoolyard doing playground duty in the lunch hour, "to ask you away for the weekend."

We pause and watch small boys bully other small boys. One cherub face comes up and slips his hand chummily into that of Mr. Bonsey who is distracted by this and can only bend and pat the sunny thatch of the kid. Ice gray eyes gaze upward.

"That's the boy," Mr. Bonsey says. "Off you go now, Harry."

"You mean?" I ask.

"Yes, of course."

"Oh," I say. "Oh. I have never."

We pass Harry flailing around the edges of another little group. He is shouting excitedly.

''You mean you maintain the virgin state?''

Harry's words translate themselves from a distortion of cherub rage. ''I hate Mr. Bonsey,'' he is yelling to the world. ''I hate him. I'm going to kill him.''

''Ah, boys!'' Mr. Bonsey says.

We are both embarrassed.

''Yes,'' I say, feeling I should be ashamed. Does he pity me? Does he think I am unwantable?

''Oh well, then.'' Mr. Bonsey crosses over to two tusslers and prises them apart, an ear in each hand, elbowing Harry neatly as he does so.

''Should you change your mind,'' he suggests looking at me with obvious second appraisal, ''let me know.''

Why am I not excited? Flattered? Why? Is something amiss?

Unspeakable. Unthinkable. I can hardly hand out the mapping pencils for affront. It is still some time before the days one said *How about a fuck?* Only the year before I had eavesdropped on two fellow students in the college art classes—females I add—who were discussing Michelangelo's David.

''Great gear,'' one of them was saying. ''Great equipment.''

''You mean his shoulders?''

''No, stupid. His 'parts,' as they say.''

''They don't look so great to me.''

''Well, maybe. Maybe you're right. I'm trying to look at the *whole* man.''

''Are you? Actually, it's rather small, isn't it, considering the size of the rest of him. Too small.''

''Economy size, you mean! Well, I suppose so, but look, it's not . . .''

''No. But even then. I don't think . . .''

"Still, great shoulders."

"Yes. I'll give you that. Great shoulders. Biceps. Thighs."

"Right."

"Okay. All of that. But it's a pity about the other, though. I mean, size matters. Does it matter to you?"

"Only the way my size matters to them. Of course it matters. But it shouldn't really, should it?"

This conversation gives me pause, as they say. Never have I achieved conversation of such frankness with mother or school friends. I begin to list the sexual epiphanies of my life.

Home on the ranch.

I am eleven, back for school holidays under the protective thumbs-up of the Virgin Rock and am walking home from the next property a mile away where I have been visiting a neighbor's daughter also home from boarding school, when I decide to cut through the paddocks rather than trudge the dirt road that passes both homesteads and adds another mile to the trek. The tree scrub on our shared boundaries is dripping the lilacs and purples of late afternoon. I am familiar with every sheep-pad, horse-track, scrub thicket. Yet that afternoon, the landscape's subtext is one of alarm. The warning notes are inexplicable and something in the quality of the light and the silence makes me hurry.

Although this way is shorter, at once I am sorry I have chosen the paddocks rather than the road but it is too late to turn round. Automatically I pick up a stout piece of fallen branch, feeling more secure as I wave its thickness and weight about me as I walk. The track penetrates more deeply into still uncleared scrub round one of the creeklines and in a gloom compounded of leaf and water I am surprised and unsurprised, as if I have been expecting this, when the scrub crackles alive at the next bend and a man steps from the trees and straddles the path, blocking me.

Unsurprised?

My heart thuds as if it will knock its way through my chest wall as I stop dead, half-turn, falter and take another pace into terror.

Why? He's a smiling man.

I have no smiles. He's a stranger and looking back now I realize he could not have been much more than seventeen though then he seemed older. I note a soiled bush jacket whose checks blur for me above the washed-out jeans. His face, which I have carried into my present, fixes itself on memory like a stamp. Rawness, a beaky hunger and hair that is too long and uncombed. I see these things somehow and wonder how I know that the smile has the gummed fixity of desperation.

"What's the hurry?" he asks.

I cannot answer. Even the trees are fleeing. The minute I move he shifts and makes a playful blocking, arms extended as if it's some kid's game.

His smile is overpowering in its static quality. It is no longer a smile.

"Come on," he says. "Show me your pants."

He moves a step closer.

"Show me."

Only I can hear the high-pitched scream that is whistling into silence in the topmost region of my skull.

The smile diminishes until it is a mere stretch of flesh.

"Show me show me show me." He's repeating the words, softly, as one might encourage a baby animal.

I am alone here on this track. Where are grandmother, mother, aunt?

Then he misjudges. He lunges and the action unfreezes

me and I crack at the outreaching arms with my stick, hearing him yelp as the wood cracks bone before he can grab it and fling it away. But I have darted sideways into the trees, stumbling and shrieking, thrusting in and out between branch and trunk, heading for the clear pasture where the home paddock comes down to the fenceline, but never looking back, not even when I hear him crash through the bushes after me, shrieking until I reach the grass flats, gobbling and gulping and not realizing his thudding pursuit had ended long before, frightened off by my racket. When I gasped across the slope to the homestead, a safer silence swept in around me as I sucked in broken breathless glimpses of roof and veranda and grandmother outside at the kitchen vegetable patch. Within a sob of that curved weeding figure, I come to a wheezing halt and manage at last to look back at the creek gully and the trees, knowing them emptied, the leaves moving as gently as ever in the late-afternoon breeze.

The lie of it!

Grandma looks up from the tomato plants and her quizzical glance is wiped out as I throw myself on her, shuddering.

"A man," I tell. "In the trees."

It's wormed out of me and grandpa sends one of the fencers down and my friend's father rides down and later they discover it is a casual come in for the shearing season and my friend's father is too late to send him packing. By the time they reach the men's sheds he is already gone and after a time I forget. Or I think I forget.

And now I am fourteen and Bonnie and Marie, for a treat, have taken me on tour. They have engagements at country dance-halls in the Mary Valley. Our base is the Miners' Arms Hotel in main street, Gympie, a large barn of a place with His and Hers bathrooms at opposite ends of the upstairs corridor. Here I am at eight P.M., having resisted the offer to accompany my relatives while they beat out ''Gipsy Taps'' and ''Prides of Erin,'' carrying my bath towel along the hallway for pre-bed ablutions. Except for the distant sea-roar of beer-saturated men in the downstairs street bar, the hotel looks and feels deserted. No sound comes from behind any of the closed doors as I walk along this glowing corridor. It is so still, despite the surf crash of yeast, I imagine that if I listen hard enough I might hear aunt and mother whacking their way through ''Chattanooga Choo Choo'' out in the Kin Kin scrub. Their repertoire never updates. Perhaps that is why, in certain pockets of cutoff country, they are so frequently re-engaged.

Utter stillness terrifies.

Outside the twin doors of the ladies' lavatory and bathroom I pause.

The bathroom door is half open and there is no light. Perhaps it would be better to describe it as half-closed. Something makes me stop. I stand, towel carefully folded across my arm like a waiter but in boarding school manner, and wait.

For what? A force field is keeping me from that foot-ajar door.

I wait.

The corridor and the moment inflate with my tension. I could wait, withheld from that bathroom forever.

There is someone behind that door.

Why don't I turn and race back to my own room? I am frozen, not with curiosity but paralysis of will as if the chemistry of whoever it is draws like a magnet and my flesh apprehends this as clearly as my eyes are learning the bilious autumn leaf pattern of carpet.

The moment becomes huge.

I press back against the wall. There is curiosity, I admit, and anger, and I stay and the racket from the distant bar underscores the silence of this corridor with its coughless laughless rustleless rooms. I wait and into my waiting a man steps from behind the bathroom door.

The corridor becomes the bush track but this time it is different. The passageway is a desert of light, I am older, larger and the man is a gabble of excuses. I don't hear them. He is gone into the corridor blaze before I have even seen his face and in seconds I have slammed into the bathroom with the door bolted before reaction sets in.

"A man," I tell Bonnie at breakfast next morning, "in the bathroom."

"Lucky you," Bonnie says, busy with marmalade.

I am too young for her cynicism and her amusement dies in the face of my appalled tears. For the first time in years that night I sleep in mother's bed, snuggled up to her late-home side, her arms cuddling me in a too-late circle of warm flesh and safety, her breath and mine mingling right through the night.

Hi, Bonnie, a different drummer, we never did mingle much, did we?

Time moves. I stay still. A lot of people believe this. I stay still in the teaching—is the word "profession"?—though the hierarchy moves me on.

Goodbye Villa Marina. Goodbye May and busdriver husband, Reg. Goodbye Mr. Bonsey for whom my time was never quite ripe. Goodbye, for the moment, Bonnie and Marie, *vale praetores!* And hello Deep Creek, hello Mrs. Moody, pub manageress of the Deep Creek Billabong, hello fellow boarders and school. Hello hello hello.

The town has one main street crossed by the railway line. There are three shops and the hotel whose proprietor is concentration-camp blonde, stunningly groomed for a one-cow hamlet in the mulga. After dinner at night she serves in the bar, flaunting her bust in a paralyzing electric blue silk. Her accent is fully and plummily English, southern counties. You know she will never say "bum" even though she understands every function of the posterior like an expert. There are four other permanents besides me and perhaps because of my sex I am seated at a separate table where I am crushed by my isolation and the deep browns of the room. Photographs of horses and dairy cattle dominate.

At the other table sit the forestry officer, a sly young man with a foxy face who works in the bank, the local butcher and a logger. Within a week I will be granted the company of a visiting forestry inspector. Each morning we exchange nods and I listen to their unvarying breakfast orders as I munch my bacon and eggs. After a week or so they add words to nods: *have a good day? Bit hot, eh? Bearing up? Kids behaving?* This is a very small town. I don't mind. I prefer it. I enjoy the high-gloss safety of my room with its jam jar of banksia, the votive offering of one of my pupils, wilting in the summer night. I am turning into my own center.

As I sit upstairs after dinner marking homework books, I hear from the barroom below through the drinking frenzy of loggers in town, the itinerant piano-tuner playing "Sentimental Journey," the notes limpid as toffee drops. There's nowhere to go from this place except one stop west into the heart of the pines or six stops east to a slag-heap mining town. The toffee'd nostalgia from the bar melds nicely with my mood in this milky-green room from whose open doors

I can see the brief strip of blacktop angling past two of the three shops, the post office cum bank and the rundown picture house where kikuyu grows between the galvanized walls and timber floor that don't quite meet, sending out runners towards the canvas bleachers.

Sentimental Journey. For—sooth! Nevertheless I tap an ironic foot and hum along and squeeze out a tear as the sprays of bottlebrush droop on the dressing table and powder its surface with fine red hairs.

The piano turner discovered at breakfast is tubby and jolly and can hardly wait to get back to the city. He has, he tells me, four more pianos on outlying farms to attend to. The newly arrived forestry inspector listens to our conversation with lines of disapproval about his mouth. I am an object of speculation. I am the only female guest. The butcher who sleeps three rooms away and faces me each day at every meal from the safety of another table will soon ask me out walking. Walking, for Chrissake!

Or press his thin dry mouth onto mine fifty yards east of the pub where he has followed me when I step out for air. "You're a sweet kid, Belle." "Am I?" "Yes. A really sweet kid. Come on, more like this." "No thank you. I have to get back and study." "Study! Give us another!"

A month passes. At Slagheap railway station, one weekend, I find myself locked in the lavatory with three minutes before the rail-motor leaves for Deep Creek. By climbing to the top of the door and launching myself over, I collapse into the startled gaze of a handsome young woman fixing her butterscotch coil of plaits before the washroom mirror.

"That's one way to leave," says my old schoolmate Sheridan McAvoy.

We sit facing each other in the rail-motor as it jiggles out of town past the grass-covered cinder piles and I discover that she is teaching at another godforsaken spot down the line. Sheridan played "The Rustle of Spring." She is an accomplished recitateuse, with a voice as full and assured as her playing. What was she doing now, apart from teaching?

"Getting married," she says flatly, "to an itinerant pineapple picker."

She waits politely for me to resume polite expressionlessness.

"Itinerant? Sorry, Boobs, but what do you have in common?"

"Everything."

"Everything?"

"Everything."

"Like what?"

"Don't be dreary. The lot."

"Will you go on teaching?"

"God no. Are you mad! I'll be picking pineapples as well. It's easier."

She laughs richly.

Is she still laughing, that Junoesque fruit sorter with the flash accent, the decorative clothes? Still roaring with laughter as she grubs along the pine rows? I spend the next week pondering the validity of marriage, its necessity, thrown askew by the flip attitudes of my mother and aunt. Surely, I tell myself, one must investigate a relationship with the other sex. Surely. There is nothing to investigate in Deep Creek, though I release a small sigh for the bachelor doctor twenty miles away who hasn't even noticed me. He has noticed only my infected toe, so swollen it has its own magic.

"Mmmmm," he had said, salivating as if handed a rare gem. "Let's—um—see. Sorry. Mmmm. Well, that's a toe and a half, isn't it? Now let me see what we can do about that. It really is quite magnificent."

The fool lances it, forgets to give me antibiotics and I end up in Slagheap hospital for a week. Returned to Deep Creek, an enfeebled hobbler, I discover that the shared bath has distributed my bacteria with horrible results. The butcher has a boil on his nose. The forestry officer has one on his right buttock. I sense general resentment. This takes an odd form.

Another week passes. It is Saturday morning and I lie upstairs, my body twisted with period cramps that make me want to vomit. Overhead, November heat is whacking the pub roof and *I'm gunna make* . . . the drinkers bellow below me as Mrs. Moody hits the barroom piano, *a sent-a-ment-al journey*. Downstairs Ellie bangs the luncheon gong and my stomach contracts at the thought of the horsey dining room, the slabs of beef, the troweling eating technique of the bank clerk.

Pain bends me double. I crawl beneath the eiderdown and wait for the spasm to pass.

A sent-a-ment-al jour-ur-nee home, they are all singing.

Two rooms away Mr. Forestry Inspector's door opens and closes in response to the gong and as his food-bound footsteps near my room, I call out. From where I am lying I see his polished dome of a head poke round the door, on his face a curious patina of phlegm rather than sympathy as he stares at me curled up with my face projecting wanly above the covers. Perhaps I don't look wan. I feel wan.

Mr. Forestry Inspector is on loan from central office in Brisbane to reorganize management and is quietly important, filled with years and gravity. He has been placed at my table, perhaps out of pity for my solitary state, where we have spoken in a desultory way about the weather for a month. But I am about to be betrayed by my innocence, my lack of something, while cramps eat at my gut.

"Please," I say, attempting dignity from a supine position, "would you please tell Ellie I'm sorry but I won't be down for lunch. I'm not well."

His face enlarges. He comes round the door and closes it gently behind him, his smile unbelieving. I say, "Please. Please tell Ellie."

He doesn't appear to have heard me. His face is impassive. Why doesn't he leave? Why does he stand there, now serenely smiling, as if in disbelief? He has the message. It is the wrong one, I realize suddenly, adding supineness to bed and aggregating too much altogether, for his face, seraphic with unexploded opportunity, gazes unblinkingly. Then he pads across to the bed using his smile like a walking-frame and leans over me, propping himself with a hand each side, looming, so that I am trapped between fleshy clamps. His voice deepens remarkably when he speaks.

"Now, what's the problem?" he demands gently, still smiling.

I repeat my message. I am beginning to feel foolish. Any moment now I will begin to shout.

Look, I want to reveal, *beneath these covers, this dressing gown, I am fully clad, do you see? Do you see? I did not . . .*

"All you need," the thickened voice decides gently while one paw removes itself from the eiderdown and comes to rest on my flinching skull, "is a bit of loving."

Is this really the kindly and rather aloof fifty-year-old with whom I have compared cloud cover and humidity at breakfast and dinner?

I thrust my body more deeply below the coverlet, dragging it up until my shamed face is covered and cry in a muffled fashion, "Don't! Don't! Go away!"

I cannot believe this is happening.

He tries pulling at the eiderdown. By now he is seated on the bony edge of my bed and the two of us engage in a silent tugowar as I drag against him like a child. The piano and the belting choruses have long since stopped. There's a smell of roast meat seeping through the fanlight. Word less we struggle for another minute with a kind of idiotic quiet violence when suddenly he desists and straightens up as if good sense has intervened. Or the smell of roast meat. Formally he asks, "May I send you up a cup of tea then?"

My humiliation is so profound I am incapable of answering. I shake my head and keep my face muffled until the door opens and closes, yet a week later he is to pin me for a kiss with a tongue like felt against the corridor wall, taking me by surprise between dinnertime and bed; and a week after that Mrs. Forestry Inspector joins her husband for a brief and beady-eyed holiday visit and breakfast weather forecasts cease as we sit silent and aloof as if never, never. He is invited to dinner at the headmaster's house when his wife vanishes and he chats on the porch as if kisses wouldn't melt in his mouth.

His summation of my needs could be correct. I am lonely and bored in this town which ticks beside a creek of treacherous water-holes, imitation rapids and pine forests that involve it in a spurious resinous comfort. Boredom. Boredom. Into which mother steps to spend midweek with me on her way back from a weekend dance-fest near Slagheap. The pub's primitive conditions amuse her. Mrs. Moody in a moment of pique has locked the one upstairs water closet, preserving the key to its comforts for casuals. Mother, as relative-guest, fails to come within this category and at night we stumble about the dark pub yard, tripping over drunks and coiled lovers.

She sits opposite me now giggling in an irresponsible fashion on the extra stretcher they have rammed into my narrow room for these few nights. It is almost impossible to move. We have just returned from the local picture show where, lounging in the bleachers, we listened to Hurd Hatfield play Chopin menacingly and say to Angela Lansbury, "It's called 'Prelude'!" threatening her virtue with innuendo. Our veins also thrilled.

"The twenty-fourth," Bonnie says as we stare at each other in the confined space of my room. "I can still play it. Shall I go down to the barroom piano?"

"Oh God!" I say. "No."

"But darling, don't you ever play it? What do you *do* all the time?"

"Be," I suggest. "Simply be."

We watch each other carefully.

Where is Marie?

"Melbourne," Bonnie tells me with an attempt at carelessness. "She's thinking of moving there."

South? South is inconceivable. No one moves south.

"It's awful," Bonnie gulps suddenly, and bursts into tears.

I sit beside her, reversing our roles, give her a hug and rub my face against her wet one. This is only the second time we have been forced for comfort into each other's arms. The irony is not lost on me.

"It had to happen, I guess. The day had to come." I find I am patting my mother's shaking shoulders as if she were the kid. "She was a lousy pianist anyway."

"Don't talk about your aunt like that," Bonnie says between snuffles. "She gave pleasure to hundreds."

"Hundreds of what?"

Bonnie giggles through her soggy makeup. Outside doors open and close. There is a listening quality about this upper storey. Someone bangs into the bathroom off the back landing and there is the sound of a tap running.

"Listen," Bonnie says suddenly, her eyes glistening through tears like a naughty child's on the verge of recovery, "cheer me up. Let's do our party trick."

I should explain that this is a musical nonsense we devised one airless summer at Villa Marina. It involves a duet, a voice-blend one semitone apart, calculated to clear a room in minutes.

"Not here, mother. Please. Not here. It's after eleven and the whole pub will hear us."

"Great!" she says. "Great! Go on. Take a note. What will we do?"

"You're crazy. Truly. Did I ever tell you what the kids at school used to call you and Marie?"

"I don't want to hear. Come on," she begs. "Please. It'll cheer me up. God, I need cheering up. Let's do the Brahms lullaby. Please, Belle."

She looks at me all wet-eyed. The hell with it, I think, and grudgingly sing "ah."

"Lower," Bonnie orders.

I drop my "ah" a third.

Her face shines with pleasure.

She sings "ah" a semitone above me. Then, "Keep singing," she says, and joins in.

"It's terrible."

"Lovely," Bonnie says. "Let's get our disharmony perfect. It says something about what I'm feeling. Aaaaaaaah."

The nighttime stillness of the rooms along the corridor is palpable. Everyone is tucked up for the night: Mr. Forestry Inspector, Mr. Bank Clerk, Mr. Butcher, Mr. Logger. The local policeman who is always locked into the bar after official closing time has by now fallen asleep in Ellie's bed.

"Right," Bonnie says. "That sounds the perfect choice. Come on now, I'll count us in." (There are praetorian overtones here.) "Are you ready? Uh one uh two uh . . ."

And off we soar, a perfect halftone apart:

Guten Abend, gute Nacht,
Mit Rosen bedacht,
Mit Näglein besteckt,
Schlüpf unter die Deck:
Morgen früh, wenn Gott will,
Wirst du wieder geweckt.

And it *was* funny.

Halfway through these dissonances laughter overcomes me and I roll round on the nasty little bed while mother pleads between splutters, "Second stanza, Belle. Second." And we rally for *Guten Abend, gute Nacht, von Englein bewacht.*

I am captivated by rebellion. We move on to Schubert's "An die Musik" and I am waiting for the banging on the wall to start but Bonnie says, "They think we're in tune, darling. They love it."

The egotism of our behavior! I confess to these things wondering if here lies some explanation of my later obsessions, my attitudes.

We perform a bracket of the most heart-tearing airs we can think of, pause for composure in the now electrified quiet of the Billabong Hotel, and then I say, inspired, "Let's do "The Rustle of Spring." No words. Just 'ah.' "

The suggestion switches mother off.

"No," she says firmly. "No."

"Why not?" Can the rest of the corridor hear us arguing?

"I don't like to."

"Why?"

"It's . . . special. To me."

"Oh God," I cry, "do you know I once made a list of . . ."

"Bedtime," mother says firmly.

At breakfast, if the other residents appear to look obliquely at us, mother is unaware and is loud and cheerful, ignoring Mr. Forestry Inspector who is so cool I feel we might perhaps have to be re-introduced. I have no idea what Bonnie does all day while I am teaching. She has a stack of cheap thrillers she is working her way through. She goes for walks out towards the re-afforestation area. I discover later that, as well, she has been giving lunchtime bangaways on the bar piano to the delight of the timber workers and the displaced-star resentment of Mrs. Moody. "Your mother," Mrs. Moody begins once as we pass in the downstairs hall. And then she sails off leaving the matter unfinished.

In bed at night we talk, deciding not to repeat our musical delights, and Bonnie tells me she has become absorbed in the philosophies of alternative life-styles. She is going beyond alternative. The news reaches me in little jets as if this creaky conversational tap is rusty from non-use. My grandparents have sold Perjury Plains at last and bought a unit on the Gold Coast and there is now nowhere for any of us to take refuge. Bonnie has decided to move out of Villa Marina. An obscene profit has been made on the sheep run and money tossed lightly left and right to mother and aunt. A small investment has been made for me. "Marie," she says, between more sniffles, "is planning to buy a terrace house in inner Melbourne" and she herself is toying with the idea of another expensive city slum in Brisbane.

After these facts settle, I realize a lot has been solved.

On the afternoon I farewell mother on the rail-motor, I announce firmly that I have no intention of remaining in the teaching profession.

"But what?" Bonnie shouts through the open window of the now moving train.

"Anything," I yell back, but she is out of earshot.

I'm misleading her. Already I had decided, even before I knew of my inheritance, and had written away, taken the first steps, applying for a librarian traineeship in a municipal library in Brisbane. As I think about it, I pray briefly, clenching my hosanna-ing hands.

"If that's what you want, dear," Bonnie says doubtfully when we catch up with each other in Brisbane. "It all sounds very intellectual."

I scream with laughter.

IV

◇

In Brisbane we try sharing an elderly house in Spring Hill.

Bonnie's eccentricities are fired by the constant flow of dropouts moving north. Is there some alternative culture map marked with a cross, for a ragtag crusade who look as if they have stepped straight across the thirteenth century *and* the Alps, nose us out, dump their backpacks and make ungrateful use of us for days on end. Guitars prop themselves against living-room chairs, occupy divans, get underfoot in hallways. The kitchen is alive with the sound of vegetables being chopped. "Vegans," mother explains cryptically. "Self-sufficiency," she chants like a mantra. Except we're the suppliers!

What about the drums, the gigs, the old-timers pining for their evenings of fox-trots, two-steps and jazz waltzes?

Bonnie purses lips and massacres zucchini.

I return home each day to a house always in flux. My center is no center. I am tired to death of strangers with user-friendly names like Stream, Sunlight, Moth, Shark. It's like living in a Longfellow ballad.

"We don't need this." Bonnie is heaving out the electric cooker. "Food tastes better cooked in the open."

"Here? Spring Hill? This minuscule yard?"

"We can try."

"But when it rains?"

She refuses to hear.

The washing machine goes next. This unsettles the transients. I find mother rubbing sheets in an iron tub she has bought at some disposal store or found on a tip. What she would really like is to be haunching by a filthy stream beating the clothing on rocks.

"God, but this is what women wept to be rid of!"

"It's the fusion of hands and fabric. The vitality of the body moving into the garments."

Where does she hear this stuff?

"Oh rubbish, Bon. Twaddle. Absolute twaddle."

"You know it all, don't you?" mother says sourly. "You won't even give another idea a chance. You're so conservative. Fancy me having a conservative daughter."

It's always the way: zanies, geniuses, whatever, breed down to the norm. There is an element of truth in the rumor that Euclid's son couldn't plot a paddyfield.

Her bed went next. Actually it went to a couple called Dreamboat and Wimps. Bonnie took to sleeping on a pallet on the floor. The good earth vibrations. Karma. Propped up by innersprings, swathed in drip-dry cotton, I can feel only guilt on my eight-inch mattress. Bonnie's satisfied snoring is enough to keep me awake.

She develops a dog. It's a vegetarian dog it discovers to its horror and when its hair starts to drop out all over the house, Bonnie assiduously collects the combings and sheddings, skilled from training in the woolsheds at Drenchings, and starts weaving small objects like table mats, egg cosies, and milk-jug covers. Red-setter place mats quite put me off eating. I begin having dinner in town. I have no center. "Never waste," Bonnie says with puritan virtue regarding the products of mange. She eyes me crossly. She haunts flea markets and late Friday night sellouts, rescuing bruised mangoes and exhausted cabbages from beneath the wheels of trucks then throws parties for twenty that are stacked with a new bumming breed of young.

Where does she meet them? Where do Stream Sunlight Moth and Shark come from?

They move in, eat, sleep a day or two, and move on.

I am the stranger in need of a center.

"Are you trying to save money?" I ask desperately. "Look, I'm earning enough for both of us. Grandma left you loaded. You don't have to do this."

Bonnie is having the power cut off next week and is gloating over a job lot of kerosene lamps dim with ancient grime it will take her weeks to remove.

"You've forgotten slush lamps," I say bitterly watching her hands caress, almost erotically, the smeared glass chimneys. "Just a saucer of oil and a bootlace."

"Don't be like that, Belle," mother says. "Anyway, tampons are more effective than bootlaces, I believe. It's the world's energy I'm trying to conserve. And it stops me brooding."

Brooding?

"Over Marie. Over the fun we used to have. I do miss her."

Aunt Marie had met a retired dredge-boat master during a weekend holiday on Phillip Island and wrote brief ecstasy notes less informative than telegrams hinting at marriage. Bonnie was in a state of panic. "She'll never come back. Never. It's over. All over. Fancy doing it *twice!*"

"You've got me," I suggest. But she doesn't hear.

If I am unable to comfort her, it is not through lack of effort even though I am aware there will be no reciprocal balm for I have my own work eccentrics to deal with and the gethsemane of home each evening in a house full of strangers (I include my mother) who barely acknowledge I am there—"Who's that?" I once heard one of them ask Bonnie, nodding in my direction. I couldn't bear to wait for her answer—a steady diet of raw vegetables and an almost bald red-setter are beginning to affect my health.

In the aftermath of Christmas festivities where we rioted on celery juice, I decide to move out. Going upstairs to bed I discover Dreamboat and Wimps who have come back for the party copulating on my bed. "Out!" I say. "Out!" "What's bugging you?" they ask. "What's really bugging you? Why don't you join us?" "You appear to have done that for yourselves," I say coldly.

I rent myself a flat six miles away as the bus flies and after the prescribed amount of maternal weepies and protest, I know we are both relieved. In another year Bonnie will sell up her urban squalor and lease a miner's acreage in the hills behind Kilcoy where she will be able, if she wants, to beat her drums to death. Nothing will be too difficult. Meanwhile I have enough to cope with: a head librarian who summons female myrmidons with a whistle and snap of the fingers, who knows the Dewey system by heart—every category—and refuses to listen to any proposed changes. A natural Luddite, computers are killing him. He furbishes his home with public gallery rejects, collects pigeon droppings and leaves them outside the building for mulch and carts the stuff off in sackfuls. Is there no end to this? It is like being back with mother.

"He's good for laughs," the underlings excuse him in the common room at morning tea break.

It should be laughable, maybe even lovable. I am beginning to worry about the validity of lovableness.

I am working in archives with a permanent smell of dust

in my nostrils, that delicate fragrance of old paper and bindings, and I have permanently swollen olfactory glands. But life is better. It's better. And as two years roll by I pass my qualifying examinations, receive a small promotion and make a circle of friends, all librarians, who have a hair-shirt quality of endurance and a gentleness the public service has never been able to damp out.

Like Seb.

In the recesses of the library stacks it was my job that month that year to catalogue all journal articles and photographs of a forgotten railhead called Jericho Flats not far from Drenchings. It is situated west of one hundred and fifty and twenty-four degrees five minutes south. I am learning to be exact in these matters.

"This is your country," Seb, the section head says, smiling his lovely smile and observing my new hairdo.

"But why? Why Drenchings?"

Seb plaits fingers and makes his smile more piercingly sweet.

"There's been a great deal of mining exploration up that way. Oil. It's possibly the biggest thing since Roma. Don't you listen to your morning news?" But he asks nicely. I think this streaky beige nonsense suits me, kills the albino look, makes me less of a negative. And I am wearing a new dress as well, color of foxed leather.

"There'll be a great deal of interest. We want to forestall inquiry by getting as much on microfilm as possible. Well, not *forestall—anticipate*. Politicians, conservationists, corporate bodies. Then there's the question of sacred sites. We have to be able to turn up something for them. The Opposition has already started buzzing around and National Heritage is interested. Even the locals will want data. Not, of course, that it will matter a damn if the government decides to go ahead. It's money that matters in this corrupt State."

"But it's all brown out there. It won't interest the greenies."

"Then you know the actual place?" Seb asks, pressing his point.

I have a smudged memory of picnic races twelve years before and Bonnie and Marie the star turn in a shearing shed streamered to kill, jammed with overdressed sweating dancers who were reeling drunkenly by midnight while I slept and woke, slept and woke, on a rug at the back of the stage. Grandma had forgotten to collect me and had driven home hours before. I was terrified to drop right off in case mother forgot me too.

The memory silences me for the moment.

There is a mass of material to be sifted: newspapers, old journals and notebooks, diaries and annotated photograph albums donated by the descendants of early settlers who find immortality in our recesses. The photograph albums engage my interest more than the yellowing pages of the *Drenchings Weekly Dispatch,* yet every now and then some obscure paragraph links itself to some faded photo and I feel the old Euclidean thrill as words and image achieve congruency.

One dusty Tuesday afternoon my attention is gripped by the posed photograph of the Jericho Flats Joint Stock Bank staff, four men leaning importantly casual against the unlikely timber walls of a shacklet, sunlight sharpening the edges of the iron roof, two trees preserved at the eastern and western margins of the picture for draft enhancement, and the faces. The faces.

There is an apparent sameness in the features of any group of people from a given social period. Fashions reduce.

Yet these four men, despite the dark suits, the vests, the chokers of ties, the solemnity of whiskers, display a certain impudent confidence, particularly evident in the gentleman second from the right, who appears amused by the very flatness of the landscape. I turn the snapshot over and check the writing on the back. He is Mr. Gaden Lockyer, teller and clerk. The year is 1874.

Behind the pretentiously titled structure—the name, Jericho Flats Joint Stock Bank has been painted roughly on a slab of ironbark—the lone and level sands do indeed stretch far away. (Shelley, you didn't know the half of it!) Not that they are visible. But sensed. Through a powerful magnifying glass that at first seemed only to raise an unwanted stippling, Mr. Gaden Lockyer's despair appears in the serif formed by his mouth, an upward quirk at one corner balancing a downward twitch at the other. Or a grace note.

All wear hats. The heat! The heat!

You know a dust-wind has just left the picture and that the rainwater tank half-seen at the rear of the building is three-quarters empty.

He was, I decide, turning the photograph down to obliterate an inexplicable jab at the emotions, interesting rather than handsome. Coincidence intervenes and within the next hour, in a pioneer's hardbound book of recollections, I find the photograph reproduced. The author is on the far left and moves me as little as his prose though I plow through it looking for further reference to the teller whose vital features compel me to contemplate here on this summer Tuesday the awful brevity of life, the temporality of the moment frozen in time on this moldering paper. That smile's owner is gone forever. Gone? Really gone? Any more than Galileo, say, or Ozymandias are gone? Or Sinding? There's a laugh.

What did Mr. Gaden Lockyer, teller and clerk, think, say, feel?

Over the months of research his face and name keep cropping up, his nimbus of importance tumescent. I am working through the larger newspapers published in coastal towns. In issue number twenty-three, volume eight, of the *Mackay Gazette,* the Joint Stock Bank of Australasia farewells him on page two. *The town,* the newspaper reports in violet phrases, *will be deeply sorry to see Mr Gaden Lockyer give up the position of assistant bank manager that he has handled so capably for the last two years, following his transfer from Jericho Flats. Our loss,* they write, *will be farming's gain, for Mr Lockyer has decided to take up a lease some fifty miles out, where he intends to raise cattle. The bank staff will miss his inspiring presence* (I giggle between sneezes), the newspaper records, *and as a token of their good fellowship over the years have presented him with a cowhide tobacco pouch handworked with his initials.* Their warmest wishes would accompany him.

Mr. Lockyer is photographed holding the pouch.

Between forefinger and thumb.

There is more.

At the farewell supper following the presentation, the *Mackey Gazette* reports, to my fascinated eye, that Mr. Gaden Lockyer, whose fine baritone has been much in demand at local soirées, delighted the guests by rendering a bracket of two numbers. "On Wings of Song" and the "Farewell" from Gounod's *Faust.* Miss Emily Watson, from Spillaway Station, was a spirited accompaniste.

His name graces district reports. Five years pass. There he is hectoring a gathering of graziers, and on another occasion I find him perched, quite some years older, on a makeshift rostrum outside a country School of Arts (where are you, mother?), haranguing a crowd before a state election. Everything in the picture appears makeshift. Someone in the mob has raised a fist that threatens near the crumbling margin. Mr. Lockyer must have missed out in his bid for political credence for a later issue of the *Gazette* reports that he had failed to win his seat by two hundred and three votes. "Sorry," I find myself whispering. "Sorry."

It is another weekly broadsheet in a town not far east of Drenchings that brings him to light again. Ten years have passed for him. Three days for me.

Mr Gaden Lockyer, the half-column reports, *of Upper Walla, has been elected councillor for the Wallabilla Shire. Mr Lockyer, who was born in England, came to Australia with his parents in 1857 where his father took up a small selection in the Upper Dawson area. Subsequently the Lockyer family moved south where Mr Lockyer senior ran sheep on a property outside Condamine. Mr Gaden Lockyer was educated at the Condamine provisional school and a private boarding school in Brisbane. He is a family man interested in the problems of rural communities and actively involved in Labour politics. His wife is active in country women's affairs and is well-known in Walla Shire for her work with the Walla Hospital Board.*

Mr Lockyer has two sons and one daughter.

Married? Spliced?

Have I missed the notice? No one has yet got *me* to the church on time.

Piqued, I shelve all other work for two days and finally, in the social page of a Brisbane newspaper, run to earth a joyless photograph in a page of similarly joyless photos: Miss Betsy Boyett, long-facedly posed, the verticals of tulle veil paralleling the lines of her cheek, beside quirky-mouthed Mr. Lockyer.

Betsy is pretty, I concede, in a wretched kind of way as if already she knows the workload of the country wife. Her eyes are enormous and lost. The lower lip, if only the granulations of print might move, would tremble.

God, I say. And I move my spyglass back over Mr. Lockyer's abradingly carved features, lingering on somber eyes and curved mouth with a jealous irritation. Why jealous? Do I really feel him to be my discovery? I refuse to believe I am experiencing reactions of this sort. Insanity.

Years pass with every hour. The piles of newsprint grow. The ransacked boxes of settler memorabilia, with their curling photos and fading ink annotations on the flip side, pile up. There he is again, kindly positioned in time by a reverent hand (could it be Betsy's?): 15th March, 1894, outside a settler's hut on his run west of Mackay. That spring bride has worn a little. There's no sign of orange blossom. She's pregnant again despite a family roll-call of three, two boys and a girl, the youngest child in Mr. Lockyer's arms. The family dog is trying to leave the picture and from behind the lean-to cookhouse a pig and three chickens are entering. Wretchedness. Struggle.

Oh Mr. Lockyer, has it come to this?

Between delicately turning the ocher pages of one hundred and fifty-three issues of the *Drenchings Weekly Dispatch,* groping through boxes of family photographs, plumbing copies of the *Mackay Mercury* and *Gazette,* the *Brisbane Courier* and the *Queenslander,* and making several hundred foolscap pages of notes later to be transferred to entry cards, Seb and I begin a relationship of sorts. He takes me to plays and concerts and gallery openings and lobster dinners at the Gold Coast where my virginity submits at last to his fifteen years' seniority in these matters. Thinking I might at this point find my missing center we achieve a quiet marriage attended by four other archivists and six cataloguers. Mother attended the wedding but in a plaster cast. She had broken her leg falling from the roof of her bush hut as she cleaned the gutters. Then we go away for a fortnight to the Barrier Reef where sibylline rains for seven days fail to prevent a sunburn so extreme Seb is forced to practice continence during the second week to avoid my cries of pain. But my nose unblocks.

Years later Seb would accuse me of courting sunburn deliberately but then, in the tropic ritz of the honeymoon suite while he resentfully patted calamine onto my blistered shoulders and thighs, I thought to woo him with innocent confidences. My virginity had startled him enough. I tell him about the man on the track and even as I tell, the terror hits me again and I whimper and pretend it's my sunburn. Seb is juicing for detail. He has begun licking his lower lip, an unpleasant habit I've noticed when he is about to receive the sunburst revelation of prurient gossip.

"And then?"

"He told me to pull my pants down. And all the time smiling. A sort of fixed smile."

"And?"

I look at Seb's face and I decide to varnish the story a little. "I said pull down your own, buster, and give me a look."

"Well, that's a new twist."

"It sort of stopped him," I say. "He wasn't expecting it. So I kept yelling *Show me, show me,* and he began to back off. *Silly cow,* he said. *Silly cow*. But I was back in the saddle by now—did I mention I was riding?—and I taunted him. *Go on, go on,* I yelled. *Bet you've got nothing* and then I dug my heels in and my horse sprang forward, practically on top of him and he just managed to jump clear, screeching at me."

Have I overplayed my hand? Seb is peculiarly thoughtful. His calamine-slapping hand has a sting to it. I want commendations for bravery but Seb says, "Quite the little ball-breaker, weren't you?"

I cannot believe I am hearing this. I had hoped for encircling arms, nuzzling reassurance.

"I was eleven," I protest. "Eleven. I thought you'd applaud."

Seb doesn't answer.

"You mean I should have *let* him? Protected his ego, his bloody *needs?*"

Seb is still silent. I inspect him. Puffy, I can see now, in his godawful crocodile motif pajamas. Puffy, not cuddly. And that smile. Well, I must be honest. It is lovely but it surmounts the beginnings of jowls, and lower down a beer gut from academic drinking sessions in libertarian pubs—the Regatta Hotel gut. His eyes are too large with a tendency to hyperthyroidism, the whites clearly circumscribing each freckled iris. They definitely bulge. I had hoped the excess of thyroid indicated an interesting sexual drive, but I've been wrong there too.

Seb is muttering something and I catch the words,

"You belittled him."

"So?"

"Well, you said he was only a kid."

"I don't believe this! My God, there has to be an antonym!"

"An antonym? For what?"

"Ball-breaker. Careful, you're hurting. Crusher. Whatever. How about womb waster? Boob buster?"

"Keep trying," Seb says indifferently, his smile now at its most outrageous. "You'll luck up on something. And if you use if often enough, you'll give it currency. A spurious currency. But currency."

"You bore me," I say unforgivably. We have been married a mere six days.

"I'm going out," Seb announces, removing his hand and screwing the cap back on the calamine bottle. He peels off his pajamas, drags on shorts and a sweatshirt and slams out of the honeymoon suite.

I am left there for three hours until the bar closes to brood on the delicacy of male sensibility, its capacity for easy bruising and the non-existence of its converse in the face of the male put-down. I wish I had thought of slamming out instead but it hurts to walk. Bonnie is right, I tell myself, in her committed obsessions, attached emotionally only to the abstract problems of life-style or drums or even me in a tangential way. As far as I know, my father had been the only man in her life. Her circle has had several centers. I wonder about the emotional refutations of Euclidean assertions and vow to give myself up to archival relics that are beginning to assume for me a reality and an importance my own days lack.

If going forward is disaster, I have no alternative but to go back. I have to start somewhere, go somewhere. Heading for the womb and beyond.

Do not put anything down this toilet you have not eaten first.

Bonnie is the mistress of précis. She has taped this message to the wall of the shack's dunny. I call it a shack because the abandoned miner's lease she has purchased sports a three-room hut leaning away from the coastal wind and threatening to rejoin the bracken floor of her scrub-forest acres. The flush john fed by gravity flow from a tank is an unexpected nicety.

We are visiting, Seb and I, and are locked into the first shocked harmony of our marriage. Bonnie's leg is out of plaster and she has an interesting limp. I worry about her. True, the view is stunning. The houselet is perched on the edge of an escarpment that watches the country unroll in superb pleats and tucks for miles. True, the nearest township is creeping ever closer to her property because of developers crazy for subdivision, but the overall impression is of isolation.

Bonnie has the same dog and now two hens as well. The three animals have unlimited access to the house and accompany her when she drives to town for mail or to stock up on groceries she cannot avoid buying. The smaller hen sits on her shoulder as she limps from one store to the next.

"She's very fierce, aren't you darling?" Bonnie asks the hen droolingly. "Thuck thuck thuck."

We have been here for two days now and Bonnie has shown us every corner of her land. Exhausted, we are collapsed in homemade deckchairs when Seb says, unexpectedly compassionate, "You don't have to stay here, Bonnie. You can move down with us, you know."

I suspect he wants her as a talking point at parties. He adores the freakish. I am part of his collection. Now that he is upwardly mobile, as they say, and has become deputy librarian, our house vibrates each weekend with the resonance of academic jousters. Everyone is a critic. No one is a performer. I long to hear kindly words spoken. I tell this to Seb petulantly after a trying Sunday afternoon when I spent my social time washing glasses. He wants my mother there to *perform*.

But Bonnie grins delightedly. "You'd hate it."

"Of course I would," Seb agrees, taking the wind out of her sails and grinning back, "but it might be fun. How about a cuppa, Bon?"

Bonnie has been snapping twigs for the old fuel stove she bought from a demolished settler's hut in the next valley. The pot rings are rusted, the oven door won't close properly, the damper doesn't work and the shack fills with smoke.

"I thought you'd be rubbing two sticks together," Seb adds, fanning with the *Observer*.

"I would," Bonnie says, "only you're so impatient. I hate," she adds, "to hear cracks like that from a barbecue freak."

Bull's-eye!

Seb, high priest of the weekend barbie, winces in his expensive casuals. His garden rituals of salad tossing and steak turning never extend inside the house to the kitchen where at mealtimes he becomes abominably limp. For a man of the eighties he has a disposition to the cultural domestic arrangements of the last century, and I am becoming increasingly soured of a relationship that sees us both travel to and from work together and sees me go on working solo once the front door has slammed. Ploys like after-work drinks with women friends fail. He can always outstay me. I try heading straight to the garden to pluck listlessly at weeds but darkness and mosquitoes drive me in; or playing sick *(I have a bit of a headache, too, old girl. Let's not eat. It will be good for us. Nothing like judicious starvation)*. Seb's cunning is boundless. No wonder he's the deputy librarian at forty with a five-figure mortgage that is grinding us both to pieces.

After three days of Bonnie's raw salads, mountain water (Seb develops gastric problems), leech and tick bites, Seb announces our return to the comforts of town. I am offended for mother. We are on our four weeks' annual leave and although she is an eccentric of talent, she is still my mum. I jolly that fact along by saying the words aloud to myself for their cozy sound. I am trying to make her my center but nothing seems to work. Despite that, I hate to leave her in her crazy comfortless commitment. The two of us, Bonnie and daughter (you note I refrain from writing "mother and daughter" at this point) go plodding up the mountainside in gumboots seeking privacy from the deputy librarian.

She looks at me squintily. "You're not happy, are you?"

We are cleaning yabbies out of our small holding tank at the spring. Bonnie has forgotten to bring gloves—or decided we don't need them—and it is unpleasant work.

I counter with vagueness. "Well, it's marriage, isn't it?" adding unkindly, "You should know." She ignores that.

"I should have stopped you," Bonnie complains. "The tiny pedant."

"You were never around."

"*You* left *me,* my dear," she says.

"Oh this is pointless, arguing. Pointless."

I must admit I do know of some sturdy and pleasant relationships. I meet couples who are still affectionate and considerate even after decades together. It's these newer couplings that abrade and dissolve within weeks months years. Grandmother blames the new independence—she means women's—and maybe she's right. They're rejecting the chattel status that's been expected of them for so long. I say this to Bonnie who, despite being a living example of this emancipation, purses her lips as she gazes back down the hill at the just visible askew roof of her shack where it skulks under trees. I gaze with her and at this distance Seb's garden-prowling figure, spotted in glimpses as he noses critically about the vegetable patch, emits, even up here, a diffusion of impatience and irritation. We watch him go back inside and reappear with overnight bags. Any moment he will begin honking the car horn to summon me with infuriated morse.

Bonnie starts laughing to herself.

"What's up? I don't feel much like laughing." I was hoping for a concentration on my own problems for once.

She giggles a little more before she replies.

"Gloombug! Don't let him worry you. Listen, I've developed an admirer. Despite all my vows."

My raised eyebrows prod her on. I won't indulge her by asking questions. What about *my* plight? I scoop a resentful pile of sludge from the tank and heave it into the trees, only half-hearing mother's account of a neighbor from the next valley.

"Nothing carnal, dear, in case you're wondering. Nothing like that. It's a tea and conversation program."

From the babble of description I pluck a name, "Stanley." Mother is busy explaining that he dislikes diminutives.

"He's a widower, Belle, of about sixty. Just a nice age for me. And he's been farming here for the last thirty years."

I fear he might be a redneck oaf but I manage to tell her how pleased I am and ponder what the sociologists describe as the oppositional or complementary aspects of gender. Christians have a terrible duality to deal with when confronted with the body—the spirit and the flesh at tugowar—but even that is not as laughable as the casuistry of Eastern religions—explaining away their dependence on sex as relaxation (''it's contemplating each *other's* navels,'' Seb tells me)—or the Muslim tralala I heard some mullah pundit in full explicatory cry give out on a national radio program: ''The junction of these two oppositions,'' he said gently and persuasive pervasive, ''finds its fullest moment in intercourse.'' I think he meant in the sight of Allah. I get really irritated when religion tries to give mystique to people wanting to have a fuck! (You notice how marriage has coarsened me.) Then he went on to say that genital differences were given the world purely to achieve this junction. I'd always had the unpopular idea genitals were for breeding and perpetuating the species. But I guess if you're an Eastern guru you can get away with anything.

''Well,'' I say to mother, ''it's good you've got someone close you can call on in an emergency. It's great. I won't worry nearly so much.''

If mother has been lonely, she's not admitting it and if she has been fearful at times as she must be when the moon opens up the secret places of the scrub and sends shadows scurrying, she has always pretended that the world is sweetly safe. She's wrong, of course, and I am beginning to feel cross about it all, about the hours I have spent worrying on her behalf, about her oddity stuck here in a clearing ten miles from the nearest township.

I make a snap decision. I want to inspect this new messmate. ''Let's go back down and tell Seb to drive back without me. I can get myself home by train later in the week. There are things I've got to talk through.''

Bonnie's eyes light up. Her lashes blink rapidly over that still intense blue. ''Now you'll be able to meet Stanley,'' she cries delightedly, my own problematic marriage the last thought in her head. "We'll drive over there after Seb's gone."

◇ ◇ ◇

Bonnie was lying.

Stanley is indeed sixty and a widower but he is no farmer.

He is an elderly dropout in a turn-of-the-century farmhouse—what the real estate jackals call a "classic Queenslander"—postulating its charms on a small green hill overlooking the river. The return verandas are draped in jasmine and Chinese honeysuckle and though it all looks conventional enough externally, the interior provides shock. Every partition has been partially or totally removed, the remaining structure braced by massive studs and crossbeams so that ultimately the house is one enormous room with arched annexes for sleeping and cooking. The rest of the space is given over to easy chairs—Stanley, I discover, does a lot of sitting—and shelving that contains the largest record collection I have ever seen. Rack upon rack of old standards, LPs, discs and tapes. As well as the latest hi-fi equipment—compact-disc players and banks of speakers—there are several vintage turntable machines, one with an enormous exponential horn. Only the terrier is missing.

Stanley presides over it all in an unhurried way, even in the initial flurry of meeting, a seemingly absentminded man with a scholarly stoop, lank white hair and exhausted good looks. But the noticeable feature, the stunning feature really, is the baby bland innocence of his eyes which are of a crystalline blue and have the wondering look of eyes seen peering over the edges of prams and strollers.

Mother is waiting for my reaction. I muffle it.

While he makes coffee, I inspect the shelves, my archival glands working at top strength. He has everything, I estimate, on my first and necessarily cursory peerings. And often several versions of everything. The recordings and tapes range from the Victoriana of music halls through jazz, rock, pop to standard classics, collector's items of baroque, rare masses, Gregorian chant, the most avant garde of serious work. There is a beautifully filed catalogue in one corner of this great barn. I pull drawers and flick through index cards. Is he simply a collector? There are tapes of Eastern music, African drum rhythms, Pacific singsings, Aboriginal corroborees. There's flute music from the high Andes and guitar music from the Basque region. Is he simply a collector?

My attempts at reconstructing or revivifying Mr. Gaden Lockyer seem amateurish.

"There's one thing you've missed," I can't resist saying as he puts the coffee tray down on the table. But I say it with a smile. I can hear my own foolishness clang.

He looks over at me with those absurdly innocent eyes. "What's that?"

Is he affronted? Anxious? Does he detect my meanness of spirit? "Trucking music."

"Trucking—music?" He is frozen into perplexed recall, the sugar bowl tendered at an oblique angle. He stands for so long like this I think he has forgotten me.

"Let me see," he says finally at the very moment Bonnie reproves, "Stop your nonsense, Belle."

He has forgotten us, forgotten the coffee. You can hear him racking his brains while he remains, defying gravity, leaning gently forward into space, the sugar bowl still extended. I take a mug from the tray and help myself to sugar but he doesn't notice.

Then he gives his head a little shake and seems to bring himself to.

"You're right. You're absolutely right. I was trying to remember. There's a box of stuff out in the shed and I thought maybe . . . no . . . you're right. My word, Bonnie, what a sharp one, eh!"

He fumbles about, sugaring his own coffee, slopping it over the sides and stirring endlessly. "Very sharp," he keeps muttering. "Very sharp."

I feel he is upset and that somehow I have offended.

"Play us something," Bonnie urges, to distract while frowning at me to be nice. "Go on, Stanley, play us something."

He clicks back into the present. "What would you like?"

"Anything dear." (Dear!) "Whatever you pick will be lovely."

" 'Rustle of Spring,' " I suggest brightly, ignoring mother's eye.

Stanley's baby orbs graze across mine. "I've half a dozen versions," he says, "including a tape taken off one made by Claudio Arrau nearly thirty years ago in New York. It's not official," Stanley continues. "Someone made it at a private party. A friend of mine took a copy when he was in the States five years back. It's quite a collector's piece."

Bonnie is gulping her coffee noisily and angrily.

"That should be interesting," I say watching him move without hesitation to the exact spot on the right shelf on the right wall. What a cataloguer! "But any will do. Really. By the way, I once made a list of . . ."

"That will *do!*" mother interrupts exerting authority for a rare once.

"You said *any,*" Stanley says. To my horror he is winding up one of the portable players, the one with the exponential horn, checking the pickup arm and lowering it onto a biscuit-thick spinning disk. "Played by the composer," he says. "This is even rarer."

And Stanley is even rarer, I think, looking out the window to escape the horrible sounds coming from the player. Outside there is one sad cow in the home paddock, more of a pet than a milk giver. From where I sit trying not to hear spring rustle cracklingly and tinnily through the back Kilcoy landscape, I can see the cow's bleak face as it bends to munch shrubbery along the fenceline. There is no other evidence of agrarian intent although Bonnie assures me later that there is a fowl run that keeps her supplied in eggs. She plays barter with bottle upon bottle of blackberry conserve, an effortless production as most of her hillside and Stanley's valley have been invaded by the pest.

All through the performance mother frowns while Stanley watches both of us with his unblinking crystal eyes and I plait fingers hoping not to laugh. When the old machine creaks to a stop, "Rustle" dying away several tones lower than when it opened, Bonnie is beyond forming enthusiastic phrases and Stanley, an interesting smile on his face, becomes high-priestly at the machine, removes the record, wipes it reverently with a tissue, replaces it and turns from the shelves with what I was to come to know as his gift for *non sequitur*.

"This *was* a farm once," he says accusingly, swinging round on me. "My grandfather took up land here, my parents endured it and I have more or less given the whole idea of farming away. Not the place. I love the place. But I spent an early lifetime in cracking dawns, milking before breakfast and then cycling twelve miles to school to be crammed with a little Latin, a little French, a little mathematics, and enough is enough."

"Of course it is, Stanley," Bonnie soothes. "Of course it is. There comes a stage in one's life." She pauses to let us imagine what that stage might be. "It will come to you, Belle, super confident though you are in what you're doing. Mark me, there'll come a time."

Stanley lowers himself foot by foot (he is remarkably tall) into a slouching rattan chair and proceeds to roll a cigarette. His movements are finicky and precise. He looks at neither of us but inspects the narrow cylinder forming between his fingers. "It does seem, I agree, as if I'm punishing the land that punished me. Maybe I was when I first started to ignore it but it's not like that anymore. I'm just tired of bending to its will. I refuse to let it dominate."

He finally lights his cigarette and draws on it with patent pleasure, leans back in his old recliner and says, looking directly at me, "It's come already for you, hasn't it? Time for a change."

Whump!

What is there to say in reply to this un-nosy prober? Who is right. Unexpectedly I find myself, *hear* myself, launched into a passionate long-winded gust of sound explaining why I had switched careers before I had really got started on one, abandoning teaching for something so solipsistic, so passive, it takes my breath away. Bonnie's name keeps cropping up, tossed like driftwood on this flood, and out of the corner of my self-justifying eye, I can see her looking woundedly at me, blocked from inserting any refutation, any excuse or vindication of herself by my torrent of wild arguments.

"I love you, mother." I finish abruptly. "And I understand. Now."

We're both tear-shot by the time Stanley finishes his

cigarette and kills it neatly in the ashtray. He is smiling peacefully, staring at me with those fixed china doll eyes.

"But I didn't mean that. I wasn't referring to that."

"Mean what?"

"Your career. Your job."

I rise and go over to the table to refill my cup, needing time before I come to grips with this. Levelly I ask, "What did you mean?" watching the coffee bubble into my mug, adding milk, stirring in sugar, too much of it.

Stanley's eyes should have been brazen to match the words he offers me when I turn at last and meet his gaze. But they aren't. They aren't.

"I meant your marriage."

"Oh Stanley," Bonnie protests, shocked. Is this a Judas protest? "Stanley, really!" Then she casts me a look.

Later she insists she has told him nothing beyond the bare fact that I am married. I believe her and the perceptions of this stranger shake loose the last assurances I have in my precarious relationship with Seb.

I drink my coffee looking stonily past both of them.

I will not be drawn. My mind has been a nest of worms for weeks.

There is a rider to Euclid's ninth proposition in Book III which states that the locus of the middle points of two parallel chords of a circle passes through the circle's center.

Philosophically, I suppose, there is little difference between the human center that I seek and the abstract. Modern self-indulgent psychology proposes that one's self is one's center but I find the theory unsatisfying. I need a center in which I can merge. An alter-ego center. Isn't that what we all look for?

Let me tell you something.

I am looking for a one-storey town
with trees
river
hills
and a population of under two thousand
one of whom must be called Gaden Lockyer.

I have been looking for nearly a year now, mentally, I suppose, but looking. Specifically looking, that is, though the research parameters of my work, any friendly alienist would have told me, had started long before from the moment child/girl fingers began to pause in turning pages of old family albums planked down by grandmother as pacifiers in the desperate evenings of Drenchings' holiday boredom; of history books with photographic reproductions, courtesy the *Bowen Gazette,* the *Charco Herald;* and now of eighty-year-old newspapers in library reference rooms where, yellowing pages spread out on the desk, I dissect and turn as delicately as a neurosurgeon, cutting through the flesh of the past; of museum photographs of mining townsfolk, cattle-station verandas, cow-cocky huts—the whole work-team, family, whatever, in their overdressed best for the hooded man behind the tripod. I am intoxicated by photos of old Chevy trucks stuck on bump roads being rope-hauled by teams of straining bullocks; of estuary ferries carrying Model-T Fords from south bank to north, wagons dragging through river shallows, squatter gardens whose rich shrubbery mocks the unpaid black labor that has created them, farewelling streamer-clutching crowds on wharves at the most outlandish landfalls in the country and little desolate groups (even the kids' hoops are stilled) watching trains pulling out to nowhere.

The sun whacks everything aslant.

Looking and looking, I hear the mournful bloot of train and boat yowling protest in defiance of the wilderness. And I see in my mind's eye, despite mother and Stanley and the insane room, a blotched photograph of the wharf at Portland Roads, three men by the shed standing on the blue rim of tropic waters in the defiant way only pioneers stand, their relaxed yet arrogant posture a giveaway, a residue of impudence there that doesn't give a damn for the resentment of landscape.

I close my eyes against Stanley and Bonnie and the room and allow my besotted brain cells to whip up a computer program of wedlock fantasies designed to ease over the hard parts. Naively I wonder about the therapeutic effects of travel. The blotched photo had turned up in a primitively written autobiography published in 1920 called *Backblock Battlers*. The accompanying text gave me a sideways glimpse of my obsession: *Mr Gaden Lockyer, grazier, Mr Sam Turton and author await the arrival of the mail packet at Portland Roads Wharf*. So much for the explanatory note to the photograph. *Mr Gaden Lockyer,* the author of *Backblock Battlers* went on to write, *has been visiting the area with cattlemen of the peninsula. He and his companions travelled overland as far as Somerset by packhorse on a journey that took the best part of three months. Mr Lockyer, the State member for Walla, now returned to his home in Mackay, spoke glowingly of the potential of the region and of the men and women who have pioneered the more isolated parts of the country. "Distance," he said, "was a continuing problem, especially for the wives and children."* (My God, I think, as

I snuffle in the dust of seven decades, he actually gives a thought to the wives. He must have been an unusual man for the times.)

My magnifying glass had revealed little but enlarged speckling.

It was that particular photo coupling itself cunningly with the younger features outside the Jericho Flats Joint Stock Bank that was to become the *idée fixe*. For in the middle of Seb's rare and hasty embraces I had found myself speculating on the sexual manners and appetites of long-gone Mr. Lockyer. Seb had hovered over me observing my speculations.

"Penny for them?"

And I would blush.

How explain that I am living out my latest reading matter, a childhood habit carried on through adulthood (is the word "adultery"?), of nudging off to sleep with any spy coming in from the cold, planning my own plagiarized escapes that ranged from Valjean's Paris sewers and Man Friday islets to perilous train and plane flights from agency operatives of east and west?

I have always liked to make fantasy practical.

"Why the train guide?" Seb would ask, peering across the pillow. "Why the airline schedule? Are you planning on leaving me?"

"Not yet." Smile.

"Sure?"

"Look, Seb, God, this is crazy. You won't believe me but I'm trying to work out how to get from Augsburg to Lucerne with a very large sum of money in unused notes, bank it, convert it into untraceable traveler's checks and get out to Oz without leaving a footprint." That should throw him. It really is what I'm doing.

He says, "Don't put me on!"

Irritated, I say tartly, "There are operatives everywhere."

"Operatives! Operatives! My God, sweetie, you're talking crazy."

"Don't call me that."

"Call you what? Crazy?"

"Sweetie, for God's sake. It's so patronizing. Such a put-down."

"What do you expect me to be when you go on as if you're losing your marbles."

He told me later that I had stared at him sulkily for a full half minute (it really is a long time, conversationally speaking) before I replied, "I'm getting tired of the present. I want to get out of it."

He had no idea what I meant.

Bonnie is singing *I danced with a ghoul who danced with a ghoul who danced with the Prince of Wales.* When your mother is a lot more entertaining than your husband is, it gets you down to analyzing the pith of matrimony.

Stanley is smoking contentedly and radiating delight for mother has coaxed him back to her shack and fed him vegetable pie and baked pawpaws. As she washes dishes and sings, he taps one foot happily.

"I enjoy political comment," he says. "Are you a republican, Belle, or do you regard your mother as nationally blasphemous?"

Mother, I must say, is one of those lucky ones who, while exhibiting all the stigmata of the screwball, retain the distanced sense of what eccentricity is about. She can stand off, as it were, and contemplate the figure she cuts drumming or singing or simply being and can laugh at herself with genuine delight.

I envy that.

"My problem," I whisper to Stanley so as not to mar mother's rhythm and cheer, "is that I am fundamentally conventional. Maybe," I say, "I take after my father. Really, though, I am beginning to take after my husband. I feel it happening."

"No you don't," Bonnie cuts in, interrupting herself mid-song, "not your father. Definitely not. For the brief time we knew each other, I can only say he was not, repeat not, boring. Maddening but not boring. You take after your grandparents, Belle dear. Poor pets. There they are, Stanley—well, there mother is, but so wrapped up in husband memories I always feel father's presence, sitting out her days in a horrid little unit on the Gold Coast, watching the breakers bore in from the twenty-third floor, frightened of being mugged in Cavill Avenue, and spending her evenings playing bridge with three other frightened widows behind dead-locked doors with bolts, screamer alarm systems and all. As Belle said once, God's waiting room."

"And what's this that we have?" Stanley asks mildly, his baby eyes wide. "God's privy?"

Bonnie rolls about at the sink.

There is something a little unhinged about mother's laughter. I think she must be the only menopausal dope-smoker in these parts, for when she comes back from the chores patting oil into her hands ("Lissom for the drums, dears!") before settling down in front of the fire, I am not surprised to see her take the makings of crumbled leaf from a plastic bag hanging over the mantelpiece and start rolling herself a joint.

But she is unable to tempt me despite her insistence that

it would relax me. We are not parallel chords in any circle, really. Screwballs give birth to conformists. Conformity is our only defense. "You're so square," Seb kept accusing me over the paltry years of our marriage. "So damn square!" As promotion, naturally enough, eased the necessity to please work colleagues, he told me this more and more often, and somewhere near the top of the ladder he also began to assume the foibles of the head librarian and could be seen summoning junior desk attendants and reading-room staff with a snap of the fingers. Sometimes he forgot and practiced his rudeness on departmental heads.

"Don't you dare summon me that way!" snapped elderly Miss Choate, who had ignored his doggy summons for so long he was forced to cross the room to her desk. Grinning faces bent assiduously above index cards while Seb flushed deeply but more with anger than shame as Miss Choate, bolstered by a seniority of twenty years, proceeded to point out flaws in his boyish manners.

At the end of a week I return to Brisbane by a series of local buses and train and I think of Stanley and his remarkable percipience and also of Seb, but with a distance rather than yearning that strengthened in inverse ratio as the distance between us shortened.

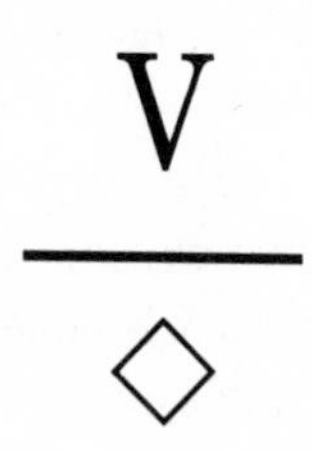

I now have a blow-up photograph of Gaden Lockyer five feet by three.

A poster firm in South Brisbane has made it for me. In this airless March afternoon with the threat of late-summer storm I sit before it, Buddha-like in the spare room. I have moved into the spare room and feel enormous freedom despite the narrowness of the cubicle and the drab view of Brisbane over the wilting shrubs in the backyard.

When I made my move Seb was furious, not because he missed my presence in the boudoir but that rumors of our geographic alienation might become gossip in the library stacks.

I have moved all my clothing there, too, my books, a typewriter and a small desk.

Mr. Lockyer broods over the room as if he, too, finds it rather small.

Seb lies alone in the double bed with his enchanting smile.

We drive to the same workplace in separate cars. I still rattle about the kitchen and cynically cook enough dinner for two but more often than not Seb's meal becomes a dried montage warming in the oven. After a month of this I begin eating out regularly.

I have started compiling a research diary and file on Gaden

Lockyer, a private project since the research on Jericho Flats finished some time ago. I am involved in correspondence with the historical societies of at least six country towns, parliamentary record departments, three coastal newspapers whose morgues I wish to mine and, on a more personal level, an eighty-year-old shearer from Dingo who has eye-witness anecdotes. These are soon exhausted. It seems there are no surviving direct descendants though I am prepared to doubt this and will shortly institute my own investigation in this matter. A line is to be drawn connecting the middle points of our parallel chords.

Why? I ask the earnestly amused face of Mr. Lockyer, now an almost life-sized bank clerk in the spare room this steamy morning in March. Why am I doing this?

Outside Seb has been driven by the height of the grass into hacking and mowing and he is dragging the mower resentfully beneath the jacaranda trees. He is determined to domesticate something and just for a moment when he pauses to mop sweat from his scarlet face, I feel a spasm of compassion. For one pure second of abstraction he forgets the mower is still running and is hauled wretchedly into the present as it ambles down the slope and begins nuzzling the paling fence. Amused, I resume my contemplation.

Should there be oblatory candles?

The clucking telephone unites us in the living room and I eavesdrop beside Seb on hearing Bonnie's strident voice as if she is attempting vocally to bridge the three hundred miles between us. Fragments of sentences come through. But what? Seb officiously ignores my grab for the receiver, waving me off arrogantly, and turns his back so that he cuddles Bonnie's words to himself.

Whose mother is she, for Chrissake?

That's the moment, the back-turning moment, when I

begin to hate him, my loathing confirmed as he clicks the receiver into its cradle and walks out into the garden without a word.

I pursue, battering with questions until he yields.

Marie, he tells me, is returning to join Bonnie, her dredge master having collapsed on the sixteenth hole of St. Kilda golf course. The ambulance taking him to the nearest hospital was redirected by casualty to another, one hour away, and he was dead by the time they wheeled him from the ambulance.

Seb pulls the mower's starter cord as if he has just read me a grocery list. I chase him across the spinning lawn and pound at his beautiful back, sobbing with rage. He knows I can't ring back. Bonnie would have had to drive ten miles into town to make that call. I sense my face screwed into new configurations.

"You look awful when you do that," Seb says coldly, heaving again at the starter cord because my attack has caused him to stall the motor.

I trail back inside and for the first time in our life together I pack the smallest, the most deliberate of go-away bags.

I'm on a spy high. Looking for the center. Another try.

It is possible for me to reach the States and be back, butter unmelting in my mouth, in one weekend.

One long weekend.

It is possible for me to nose out my conception spot in San Diego on the way back or through to the east coast. I really have been investigating the permutations and combinations of airways schedules.

The sound of my departing car is drowned by the snarl of the motor mower now munching its way around the barbecue pit. I am fled airportwards before Seb can pull the starter ratchet to Stop, bristling with passport and a visa with three years to run, credit cards and one change of clothes.

"You're sacked," Seb will, and does, pronounce when I return to work, twenty-four hours late, my eyes popping with jet lag. "Where have you been?"

I had arrived straight from the airport, my brain fogged from in-flight movies, my body clogged with airline meals.

"America," I said, walking past him and going straight to my desk.

Seb ignored what appeared an obvious lie and stalked upstairs.

"Where were you?" he asked again as we passed later in the day outside the staff common-room door.

"I told you," I said.

His jaw tendons displayed themselves through tightened skin.

At home that evening Seb, early for once, asked again but I was too far under with sleeping pills to mumble the truth for the third or even a fourth and a fifth time.

It is interesting—and I discovered this fact very early—that when you tell the truth, particularly if it's outrageous, no one ever believes you.

There has to be some sort of rapprochement for we are a social pair, according to Seb who thinks it fitting. His job demands it.

A week later here are six of us clutching after-dinner drinks or coffees on the back stoop looking across suburbia to glimpses of the Brisbane River trapping twilight's gleam on its muddy surface. There's Frank Hassler from Cataloguing accompanied by a small wide-eyed junior from a branch library. I suspect Seb of interest as well. Patch (the affectionate agnomen has been bestowed by Hassler) is given to plunging cleavage and wrinkled lisle stockings. The antithesis is stunning. And as well there are the Flutes, both academics with tenure. They often mention this. They don't often mention that they work at a technical institute and not a university. Garry Flute has been everywhere. Erica Flute has been almost everywhere.

Worn out from ministering I am sagging behind the strategic camouflage of a philodendron, limply holding a Campari and listening to the others discuss possible holiday destinations.

"Tahiti's fucked," says Frank Hassler who has also been everywhere. "And Spain. Spain's really fucked. Greece, Italy, Peru, the Bahamas, Britain. God, Britain! Fucked. They're all fucked."

"But I want to go somewhere, Frank."

Is there the tiniest suggestion of whine in Patch's musical complaint which she has transposed a girlish and plaintive semitone? "Come on, you others, where? Help."

"There's nowhere *to* go," Frank says. "The planet has become a nightmare of tourists crossing and recrossing on package tours. The whole globe is geared to the seven- , nine- , fifteen-day joy binge. Everything's fucked. Stay here. Enjoy here."

"But I've been here."

"Delicious!" Garry Flute cries. "Delicious! Been here, done this!"

"But I've never *seen* Tahiti or Tonga or Samoa. I don't *know* the Pacific."

"Those emphases make it sound so carnal," Garry Flute says.

Seb watches the four of them, his smile at its most beautiful. I find myself wishing his teeth would go black.

Frank Hassler is becoming annoyed. He reaches rudely for the decanter and pours himself another port the size of a Coke.

"If you want to be ripped off by natives just finding their tourist muscle, my dear, and dine regularly on radiated lobster, then you're mad. You'll have to do it alone."

"Anyway," Erica Flute says, "it's wrong to give even a cent to the French. And think of siguatera poisoning."

"I try never to think of it," Garry Flute says amid appreciative laughter.

Frank Hassler frowns. His first marriage has been ruptured for only two years. He is a librarian, *faute de mieux,* having tried and failed at a political career. I wonder if he would be interested in Gaden Lockyer, who knew the horror of political disgrace right at the end. Flattery in Frank Hassler's early years had got him everywhere. Pre-selected by a conservative party he went on the hustings dragging his wife behind him. He took her hand affectionately on public walkabouts, helped her in and out of cars when newsmen were around, smiled fondly into her eyes while cameras clicked. She couldn't believe this attention. "And, I might add," he would announce on one public occasion after another, "my wife is my greatest supporter." Smile smile. Her own turned into a frozen grimace. Almost on the eve of election he ushered her onstage, one arm about her shoulders, to the cheers and yoicks of a wining-dining mob of supporters to whom, after the chairman had made his introductory speech, Frank waved his gratitude before turning and kissing his wife soundly to applause and catcalls.

She had waited until the whistles and cheering died away.

"Thank you," she said. She had a clear carrying voice. "He hasn't done that for years. Seven and a half to be exact."

"For God's sake!" he hissed.

"You don't mean it, you insincere bastard," she hissed back. "He doesn't mean it," she cried, turning to the crowd. They were fascinated. "You never do it when we're alone," she said.

"Jesus!" It was turning into a public domestic.

He kept trying to catch the eyes of his minders to have her thrown offstage but she had the audience enraptured as she took a step towards them, smiled wistfully and waved in a tiny submissive gesture that embarrassed him even more.

He was completely stumped for chin-up words as she walked away. "What a kidder!" he laughed nervously. "What a kidder, eh?"

The newspapers published every detail, with photos. He polled disastrously. His wife lived on alone with unamused memories and worked at her golf handicap.

I watch Frank frowning. I watch Seb watching Frank frown. I lean forward under my green umbrella of leaves. I lean, lean, as if I am some threatening rock or tower that will collapse on the party. The eyes around the barbecue pit under the mango tree are glittering above the ruined table with the alerted interest of observers hoping for a lovers' jangle. I look from one to the other, from the Flutes to Frank Hassler to Patch but always, as if he were my center, my eyes return to Seb who is standing near the fire having trouble with a reluctant wine cork and the first of the mosquitoes. As if there had never been five years of marriage I find myself inspecting him impersonally. He has the claret bottle between his legs and is wrenching at the cork with furious twists. Bits of it fly about.

"New York's not fucked," I suggest, availing myself

of their own trendy participle. "I was there last week-end."

"Were you, dear?" Seb says smiling sourly. "Oh my God, this bloody cork." He never listens. Not to me. He hasn't been listening for five years.

"I said New York."

"We heard you, dear. Frank, pass me that other cork-screw will you, or a putty gouger or some goddamn thing."

"Eating a BLT at the Rockefeller Plaza down by the rink."

"Oh yes," Seb says, humoring the idiot wife. He has the last of the cork out by now and is pouring more wine into Patch's glass and his own. I put my hand over my Campari to protect it.

I find I am shouting—well, not shouting—but increasing my volume for our absorbed guests. "And had I lunch in San Diego."

"I don't believe you," Seb says. "Erica?"

She is too delighted to look anywhere but at me. Frank and Garry Flute lean back as if the outdoor table is suddenly too small. They are captivated by the evening's progress and even more so when I leap up, rocking a reef of crockery, and demand to know if Seb wants proof.

"Proof! Proof!"

Ignoring his sumptuous italics I walk inside, coolly, and extract evidence from the back of my spare-room wardrobe: hotel receipts, diner's checks, my stamped visa and a leather cylinder like an extra-large old-fashioned folio holder and go back to the titillated guests.

"There," I say truculently, thrusting an opened passport under Seb's unwilling nose and waving the leather cylinder about.

Seb glances briefly at the appropriate page.

"Salami anyone?" he asks. "Bratwurst?"

I hit his hostly arm with the cylinder. Frank Hassler's face is angelic with pleasure.

Seb puts down his glass carefully and grabs the leather case from me.

"And what have we here?" he demands of the world. "Souvenirs? Tourist trash? Not a wifely present?"

He opens the case and pulls out the drumsticks.

"Heavens!" he says. "A gift for mother."

"They're my father's," I say. "My father's. He gave them to me."

Even Seb composes his face into more seemly lines. A few remnants of my history have stuck after all.

"Your father's what, dear?" Frank Hassler asks, feigning ignorance.

I ignore him. I drop my eyes and refuse to look at any of them but I look at the long brown leather case in Seb's hands and feel tears prick as I reach out and grab in return and snatch it to me. Seb is holding the sticks out into the candlelight.

No one knows how to respond. I hand the case to Patch who shows some vestige of warmth as she inspects my father's inked-in name inside the top flap.

"Ooh look!" she cries, her fingers spelling out the words as if she's just mastered reading skills. "Ooh look, Frank!" She turns to me. "Is he your father?"

I'm nodding. I don't want to tell them he was a trumpet player by profession (I have never spoken of him in any detail), that these sticks were something he had bought once for my mother and she had left angrily behind. I don't want to say anything. But Seb does.

"The marvels of modern travel," he comments with his delicious smile. "I never cease to be amazed."

◇ ◇ ◇

There'd been a series of pressures.

I mean girls. Women.

"I'm sorry about that," Seb would confess, telling me. He always *told.* He believed in the healing value of confession and catharsis. Catharsis for me, that is. The first time there had been tears.

"She's nothing, really. It's nothing. Just a student. I can barely remember her name. It's nothing."

"Then why tell me? Can you remember mine?"

"What?"

"It doesn't matter."

He would sob for a bit and cling. This wasn't what my reading had trained me to expect. Men were devious and arrogant and when discovered in infidelity became angry and lied. In Seb's case it was as if admission were stimulus to orgasm, for afterwards, in the sticky connubial reconciliation, he would take my head in his hands as he thrust away and I would feel—no, I would know—he was trying to fuck my head. He was bent on turning my skull into a second orifice, establishing a thing-ness. All of me. My God, he was going to take all of me and he refused to let the brain be separate from his mindless banging. He wanted to incorporate it into the act as if the vagina led straight to the cranium.

"I know what you're trying to do," I accused him once. "Get your hands away from my head. You're trying to fuck my skull, aren't you?"

He smiled in a satisfied way, delighted I'd got the message.

"Goose," he chided sweetly. "Silly goose. You're too bright for that."

I agreed with him and his face changed from sweet to sour, light to dark.

So after girl number seven, nine, whatever, and the telephone call from mother, it was easy enough to allow him to assume I had fled up-country in a filially dazed resentment.

I reached Los Angeles only a little later than the time I left Brisbane. It was still Saturday and I was elated the entire trip that no one knew where I was, could not hazard a guess, not in Seb's or Bonnie's most fantastic conceptions, or imagine this unknown unimportant archivist cog flung into space at over eight hundred kilometers an hour towards a continent she would glimpse for a mere two days before being flung back.

The center hunter.

That was nonsense of course. Merely finding the trailer park where I was conceived would prove nothing, establish no building blocks of emotional security, but might serve to satisfy a sentimental wish to examine the connotations of my origin. The furniture, as it were. I had an address that was part of my childhood grudgingly revealed by mother, the rare cards and gifts from unknown territory, and though I knew father was long gone from there, there would be satisfaction in looking. I kept asking myself why, on a previous New World visit with Seb when I suffered for five days in Washington at an international library conference, I had made no effort then to discover father. Perhaps I had believed Seb might still provide a point of secure reference.

The cabbie dropped me at the gates of a rundown trailer park simmering in Californian sun. The woman behind the office glass was one of those obese women who can be found all over the States, huge and light-moving. Above her pebble lenses was a lot of shiny white forehead which wrinkled as she listened to my stumbled inquiry with suspicion. When I finished she told me she couldn't understand me. Fazed by my accent. I tried again and when dawn ultimately over Lethe broke, her smile was wide and sorrowing.

"Honey," she said, "that musta been alla thirty years back. No way that van is gunna be there now. No way. Why, I wouldn't even know where to look. Whole park's been changed about before we come."

I ask, a foreign suppliant, if I can wander round. I have to absorb some moment from this place after all that distance, the infinite tangent drawn to the circumference.

Her lenses flash. I don't look dangerous. I have been diminished by travel. Clothes and skin are crumpled. My hair is sticky. I'm afraid I smell, not simply of weariness but the angry despair that has traveled with me. She's dubious.

"From Australia," I retell her. "I've come all that way."

"Jus' to look at this ol' trailer park?" she says.

Who could believe this, I agree. The fruits of impulse or obsession look toxic to the outsider. I offer my passport as guarantee and she thumbs through it slowly and carefully.

"Well," she says at last, "it's so goddamn crazy I jus' might. I jus' might at that. Look," she offers, "I'll get my ol' man to show you around. Why don't you set yourself down."

She waddles into a back room where television has been making muffled cries. I am so exhausted I could drop down on the floor of this hot cube but she is back before collapse with a beanpole husband who resents being dragged from his Saturday program.

I go through it all again. It is starting to sound lunatic, even to me, and I can see by the way he looks quizzically at me, his head a judgmental fraction to one side, he thinks it's crazy, too. Loony country. He shakes his head. "What you say the name was again."

I tell him.

"Well," he says, "there's but only one ol' reglar who's been at this park the last twenty years. Maybe he knows sumpn. What you say the name of the group was?"

"Rockwarblers." I drag up a smile. It is hauled from farther down than my boots. It is hauled from a slow hot summer night on the veranda at Drenchings with Bonnie and Marie, brain-addled by reminiscence.

We trudge through the park. I know he is resenting missing his ball game. He tells me all the vans are new by now, old ones replaced over the years. "But this ol' chap," he says, "this one we'll go see, was here when I came and he was here way back before then."

We are moving between rows of fifty-foot boxes, all with their TV antennae, their patches of garden. A few kids are playing up and down the trailer laneways, biffing a softball. Everywhere there's the blare of canned music. By now we are headed towards the boundary where there are half a dozen trailers parked under a line of trees.

"That end one," he says, pointing. "I'll jus' give him a knock."

The van door opens up on a seventy-year-old with a crutch under one arm, and behind him a television set is flashing with the ball game the park manager is missing. I go through the calvary of explanation once more and the park manager nods my words along as if this gives credence to what I'm saying. I don't care by now. I'm too tired but I hear the park manager say "Then I'll leave you to it" and he's gone fast and the old man in the doorway of the trailer and I stare at each other.

"My father," I say. "Look, I know it sounds crazy, I know he's not here anymore. I just wanted to see where he lived. Where I came from. Where I came into it."

The old man says, "You're going back a long ways, miss. Quite aways back. But I remember—well—some things. Where you say you're from again?"

"Australia."

"Thought you said that. That's a helluva way. I was there for a bit during the war. Place called Townsville. You know it?"

I nod.

"And you came all this way to check out your dad? Well, I call that a real nice thing to do now. A real nice thing."

He's smiling at me and he says "Sure, I remember Huck real well. Didn't want to say too much in front of that gateman. He's a real snoop. But sure I remember. Used to drive me nuts when he and his buddies practiced at the van. We had a few words in our day. His trailer was just over there under that last fig. That's not it now. His fell apart a few years back and management bought a new one. But that was it, right there."

The sun is vertical. It's pressing me down into the earth's center where I have no shadow.

I ask if the van owners would mind if I walked over there.

"Don't see why they would," the old man says. "Not when they hear you came all that way. Hang on a minute while I get my stick and I'll walk over with you."

Lowering himself painfully down the trailer steps, he hobbles beside me along the path to the last trailer. I don't even see it. It's the space it occupies I see with my eye for emptiness. And I don't really hear him knock. It's the answering silence I hear, the silence behind the drawn blinds and the absent car.

"It doesn't matter," I say. "I only wanted to walk round this place. You see, I was conceived here, right here, under that fig, I suppose."

I walk away from him to the back of the trailer and look up at the trees and the sky through the trees. My feet are printed on mother's invisible tracks, dusted out by time, grassed over but still here in essence. Mum, I say softly, I'm here where I started. No one answers. I am lumpy with unshed tears.

The old man is waiting patiently when I come round the end of the van site. "Not much to see," he says.

"It's the feel," I tell him. "Can you understand?"

"Sure," he says. "Sure I understand. My wife was with me fifteen years then she up and left with some smartass hardware drummer who was passing through. But I still feel her around. I know what you mean."

"I'm sorry," I say.

"It's a long time ago now." He runs a hand through his thin hair and gives a crooked grin that is largely gum. "You like a coffee? Maybe I can dig around in my memory for Huck."

His trailer is scrape-clean and apart from half a dozen paperbacks and a vase with three plastic daisies, holds only the essentials: table, two chairs, a cot made up with the precision of a hospital bed. I concentrate on the daisies and observing me he says, "Never wither. I just dunk 'em under the tap. Here. How do you take it? Cream? Sugar?"

I stir in silence while he watches me. The whole noon is tinged with the surreal.

"So you want to know about your dad," he says finally. "Can't recall when I last heard from him. Ten, maybe twelve, years since he wrote what you could call a letter. You know, after your mother left, he stayed on here a few years. She was a nice kid, your mum. Bit crazy but nice. Huck used to show me snaps of you and her. When he got a card he'd tell me. It's hard to explain how he felt." He hesitates then gets up and goes over to the stove to heat up more coffee. "It was like he was happy to be a free agent," he goes on, his back turned to my probing eyes, "if you don't mind me saying that. But like he missed her as well. You know what I mean? Having it both ways, I guess, but that's human nature for you. He wasn't a bad guy, Huck. Just a bit irresponsible, maybe, and finding it hard to keep ahead of the game. He could play all right, but there weren't the jobs and there was a helluva lot of competition. Anyway, one morning about three years after your ma left he came by and said he was going up to L.A. He sent me a card now and then. And then, just last Thanksgiving, way out of the blue, I got one from him in New York. Had to work at it to remember who he was."

"Did you keep it?"

"I don't keep anything," he says. "Guess you noticed. But there was an address, somewhere in the west fifties. Not that that's much help. But I can remember this." He comes back with the coffeepot. "Like another?"

"Please," I say anxious not to hurry him.

"Well, he did mention a place he was getting gigs. Name kinda stuck—The Village Line. Maybe you could track him down."

My head is swimming. I feel I should write it down. I say the name over a few times.

I don't really want the second coffee but I feel I owe it to him and we sit there talking about nothing much. I can only repeat what I heard or I think I heard. His emptied trailer is crowded with shadows, a profusion of nothing. I leave him my name and address, aware he would keep neither, promising I'll let him know how I go, and then he walks me back to the office where I ring for a cab to take me to the airport.

My exhaustion is developing a baroque quality similar to being drugged. The fatigue grapples me into a kind of rigid paralysis that destroys memory of the flight east though I seem to recall an automaton-like changing of planes and coming into La Guardia in the evening dark, still Saturday, and finding myself a small hotel room on the east side.

Look, this isn't a detective story. I refuse to display the minutiae of search, the marginalia of tracking here and there, though perhaps the method and determination that fueled me were a by-product of my archival peerings. In any case, round midnight, revitalized by a brief doze, a hot bath and several coffees, I find myself confronting a sad stranger in a midtown jazz bar and settling for the approach abrupt between sets.

"Hullo," I say, skipping the hogwash of introduction and explanation, "I'm your daughter, Belle."

Poor man. Poor dad.

He's a spare sort of fellow with a sandy head of hair, a late-night face and gray eyes that refuse to believe me. Does he imagine I'm an aging groupie, a desperate pickup with a down-under twang that hits his ears like a foreign tongue? The rest of the band exchange winks but there's no erotic zip in my approach. I have a photo of my mother as she was and another more or less as she is tucked into my passport wallet and the belief and disbelief on his sprung face are only natural. He asks me to wait. There's one more set. I get a seat close to the group and sip a gin and lime. All through the changes, the heartbreak of those last three numbers, he is eyeing me as he plays, the voice of his trumpet illusory and cryptic. I watch him, eyes unblinking.

One hour later we are facing each other in an all-night diner. He has tucked his instrument case under his feet and forty years of not quite making it stare bleakly at me from across the vinyl. Neither of us can fumble the right phrases together. He's knocked all awry with sudden parenthood and I think I've managed to convince him of the oneness of our blood with my dozens of Bonnie and Clyde stories, the marriage legends mother poured into my unchildlike ears and a "say hello" message from his old neighbor in the San Diego trailer park.

I have his nose, I have his mouth. I don't mean to be rude but I am treating his face like a map on which I search for recognizable features. The gumchewer with the high surf behind him has gone.

"God!" Huck keeps saying. "Jesus God, what a thing! Out of the blue." Every now and then he rubs both hands across his face and knuckles his eyes as if trying to clear them, shaking memory into focus.

"Dad," I say, dropping the monosyllable so cautiously it thunks between us, "dad, this is only a sentimental journey. I don't want anything. I only wanted to know who you are. I need—needed—to know."

His eyes blink rapidly. I am terrified he might suspect me of a wild impersonation despite seeming acceptance. I am terrified he might weep.

"It's such a shock," he keeps saying. "Such a shock. Jesus! A brand-new grown-up kid straight out of the sky. Jesus!"

"I'm nearly thirty," I tell him. "You'll have to forgive my curiosity. I just wanted to see you."

''Did Bon put you up to this?''

''No.''

He doesn't believe me. I repeat my denial. ''Never.''

''Well,'' he says, ''now you've seen me.'' He makes a face. ''It's not much, is it?''

''It's fine,'' I say. ''Absolutely fine.''

We are so awkward with each other I decide that blood relationships are unnatural. We look at each other a long time without speaking and the waiter comes across and tops up our coffees and we simply sit and stare and then unexpectedly he smiles, not forced, not suspicious, but easy and open as if the whole situation is a joke.

I give him a smile back.

''You sent me a toy bison when I was four,'' I say. ''Remember?''

''Sure,'' he lies gamely. ''Sure I remember.''

''I trailed that bison all over the sheepyards till it just about fell apart,'' I tell him. ''Mother kept washing it and it got more and more faded and the stuffing lost its kick.''

''Like me.''

I shake my head at him. ''I've still got it,'' I say. ''Back in Brisbane. It's become a kind of—well, talisman. A good-luck mascot. I can't bear to let it go.''

''Lay off, Belle,'' he says unexpectedly. ''Don't pile it on.''

''I'm not. I'm just telling.''

''You're making me feel a real shit,'' he says.

That isn't what I want to do at all. I had thought I was merely piling up the evidence for this brand-new stranger father whom I rather liked the look of. I wanted him to believe in my authenticity, even though it eluded me. I fumble with my purse and look away.

''I'm sorry. I didn't mean to do that.''

I tell him about my marriage, setting it out like some comic snack for two. I draw a primitive of mother's life-style. I say, "Why don't you come for a visit."

"I can't do that," he says. "Hell, Bonnie'd hate that."

We argue that one for quite a while and I ask, "Are you married?" And, "Hell, no," he says. "I'm still married to Bon. There's been . . . well . . ."—he does hand-rolls—"a few things this way and that. You're a grown lady. I can say that. But nothing too deep. No."

We talk until three in the morning and my eyes are falling out of my head. It's minimalist stuff. Euclid was minimalist. The sheer brevity of his explication has always taken my breath away. I tell father I have to leave the next night and as I say this I cannot bear to look at him for fear of detecting relief but in the taxi going back to my hotel he turns to me sadly and says, "Can you see me for a minute before you leave? There's something I'd like to give you to take back to Bon. Just say where and I'll be there. God, Belle, this has been one hell of a night."

On impulse I lean across and kiss his weathered cheek. He smells of cheap after-shave and bourbon and this smell moves me more than anything else. I start to cry and he pats me clumsily on the shoulder as I pull the cab door open. "Hey," he says. "Hey. Don't do that. God!"

There are still people about on Fifty-fourth but New York gives one a kind of invisibility and I walk into my hotel doorway unashamedly howling.

The next afternoon we meet briefly at the Rockefeller Plaza. I'm sitting there eating a BLT and working through my third black coffee when father comes up to my table and hands me this leather cylinder. "They're Bonnie's," he says. "She forgot to take them with her. I kept them all these years. Wondered now and again if maybe I should give them back personally, you know. You've solved it for me.''

I look at him. His face has been remolded by sleep and I don't think he cares one way or another about Bonnie or me or the world beyond Manhattan. Did Euclid ever theorize about a circle with no center at all?

''Dad,'' I say, and he winces, ''come over. Come on over and give them to her yourself.''

He shakes his head. He's restless. He won't sit with me but stands edging about as if he's ready to rush for a train a bus a plane. I don't think I've meant a thing. Or perhaps I've meant too much. That's the way I'll read it. I can only write down what I hope, or think I hope.

''Please,'' I urge.

He looks at me and his eyes shift away, only microscopically, but they shift, they shift from the center and ''No,'' he says. ''Sorry Belle. No. I can't do that. But give her my love.''

Then he's gone, dematerialized, in the Sunday afternoon crowd before I can even catch at his arm.

At work I concentrate on Gaden Lockyer as a hoist, a rig, a solid structure in the dissolution of my spirit world.

Seb tries amendment tactics. In a last-ditch attempt at marital reconstruction he flashes airline tickets to romantic places junked by Frank Hassler. Stevenson once wrote that to travel hopefully is better than to arrive and he should know, given his South Pacific days. I shall depart like du Bellay's Ulysse, hoping to return home at last after *un beau voyage* but

When I come back to the *bure* on the beach at Poindimié, I find Seb trying to hump the housegirl. I say *trying.*

It was a rushed job. He hadn't bothered to remove his shirt or sandals and the sadly comic aspect of his rump, that utter featurelessness of the behind, only roused me to a state of exasperation.

"Don't stop," I apologized to the flurried clothes-pawing bodies. "Please keep going. I'm so sorry."

I quite liked the housegirl. Several times over the last few days we had talked together. She was a bright good-looking Melanesian who had come down from Ouvea for the job and was saving to take money home for her family. Her shiny giggling face peered up at me from the bed as Seb flung himself off.

Calmly I began taking clothes from hangers, folding them and packing them into my bag. Not even the sound of the door clicking shut behind the sidling Rosella made me turn. Through the shuttered window of the *bure* I could see the sparse shadows beneath the coconut palms explode under her running feet.

This had all been a terrible mistake. Motivated by that barbecue talk and Frank Hassler's challenge to the world, the febrility of this attempt to re-establish or recapture impossibilities was patent. We had stopped for the first three nights in Noumea, exploring the exotic possibilities of the town. The heat was appalling and everywhere our ears were assailed by the accents of home. There was no escape. The package tour, as Frank Hassler stated, was dominating the planet. "I don't want," I told Seb crossly, "to sit in a French restaurant a thousand miles away and listen to people from Melbourne whining for the Barrier Reef." *"C'est la vie,"* Seb said in what he assumed to be a French accent.

When we reached our resort some hundreds of miles up the eastern coast on the fourth day, the indifference of the Gallic proprietor who watched us lug our bags from the coastal bus was stunning. With only the vaguest of directions he sent us off to search out our *bure,* sauntering after us in order to explain that because the power was generator produced, all lights would be switched off by eleven each evening. His command of English was splendid.

"What if we want to read?" Seb demanded in his best French, determined to extract multiculturalism if it killed him, furious already with the blinding sea-dazzle and the scalding quality of the sun. *"Si on veut lire?"* he kept trying.

"Ah," the manager said, stroking his mustache. "Do speak English. I understand English. I don't understand your French."

"Read," Seb said crossly. "If we want to read."

The manager threw out his hands in a delectable gesture that denied all responsibility. "Not possible."

There were no fly screens either and the sandflies and mosquitoes were already attacking without waiting for the dark. The manager pointed out a stack of mosquito coils on the wall bench.

"Pour les terroristes," he suggested, making his little joke. "Every comfort. *Allumettes*. Matches, you say. Restaurant over there. Everything." His smile broadened and he waved vaguely in the direction of the beach where I had already glimpsed a large open thatched deck set out with tables and chairs. Pop music bucketing from speakers was vomitously audible, even here. The gelatinous blue sea rolled to the throb of a bass guitar.

"There is no key," the manager added as a bonus. "Valuables in my safe, eh? Passports in my safe."

"What do you mean no key?" Seb cried.

The manager shrugged. "There is no key. None of the *bures* has a key. We do not think it necessary. You're in

France now. Everything is *amical.*'' He smiled and backed to the door. ''Don't forget. Passports in my safe.''

''Like bloody hell,'' Seb muttered.

He had dumped his bag and was sitting hunched and waspish on one of the two narrow divans. He waited until the manager faded away between the palms. ''Monsieur bloody Hulot!'' he said. ''Christ! When I think of what we're paying. It makes you wonder what the cheaper places are like.'' It was impossible they could be worse.

''For God's sake let's get a drink,'' Seb said. ''I don't think I'll last the prescribed seven days in this paradise.'' Already his face and arms were coming up in small red lumps.

We put on our bathers and, coated with insect repellent and clutching passports and traveler's checks, went to investigate the bar and the beach. The sand strip at high water in the lagoon was so narrow, a prone sunbaker would extend from dune grass to water. The sea itself was a maze of coral shelves that precluded swimming and stretched shallowly for half a mile to the reef.

Seb kept scowling and scratching. ''At least we can drink ourselves into a stupor.'' He went straight up to the bar where he ordered and drank three screwdrivers without a pause.

There were no other guests except two very pretty homosexuals who were easing their sunburn under the overwhelming shadow of the longhouse roof and gearing themselves up to face lunch.

''Delicious,'' one warned. ''Le hamburger. Le grand Mac. You'll really feel you're in foreign parts.''

They had run away from Club Med, they told us. For the second time. The first time an airline steward they knew in Sydney smuggled them out to the airport when he returned on his next run to the island, but a Club Med joy leader on a Club Med bus waiting for the next package group had spotted them and made them go back.

"How could they do that?" I asked.

"Easily, dear," they said. "Easily. Threatened to make trouble with customs. Didn't want the place given a bad name."

At that point the younger of the two sprang into action parodying Club Med exercises organized to relax newcomers and get them into the spirit of the thing while his companion swung into the Club Med welcome song. They did malicious clapping action in unison. I began to feel the holiday improve.

"Then how did you get here?"

"Walked out," they said. "Late at night. My dear, we hadn't seen fresh fruit for six days. Everything was canned. We were getting scurvy. So we snuck out, walked into Newmea, as the Aussie tourists say, and booked into a scruffy hotel, which at least had authentic French grime, in the Rue Sebastopol and caught the bus up here next morning."

"But this place is bloody awful too," Seb said. *"La plus ça change . . ."*

"No dear," they said. "No. Not compared with."

We had dinner together. There were two kinds of steak: *au poivre* and *aux champignons* (canned), a pretentiously named beef stew, a reef fish ("Mmmmm!" the proprietor who doubled as waiter said, kissing fingers. *"Exquise!")* which smelt and a spoonful of melting ice cream on a *coulis* of tinned pineapple.

"Jesus!" cried ravenous Seb. "I don't believe this! Where are the native feasts, the grass skirts, the dancing girls, the island bands?"

"Not here, dear," the two fags said. "But it's a change. We don't have to do exercises."

As the sun dropped like a rock into the sea ("It can't bear the menu!" the younger man whispered), the sandflies stopped biting and the mosquitoes multiplied.

"There's no telly, no radio and the only telephone is in the proprietor's office which closes at five," they told us, "should we not survive the fish."

Seb decided to get drunk.

In the morning I left the *bure* before him and strolled north along the coast road for a mile, the sun clamped round me like a coat. The sea was gently eroding all edges of thought with the sort of hypnotic insistence that must have rendered inebriate those lost gulls of sailors who winged the Pacific in search of the ultimate landfall, the ultimate island, atoll, motu. By the time I crawled back, the music had been switched on in the bar and they were playing through their second tape. They had only two tapes and the evening before we had heard both of them four times.

In the storeroom behind the bar Monsieur Hulot was fondling the caramel brown flesh of the bargirl who shrieked with giggles as she observed me over his unaware shoulder while I waited to put in my breakfast order. The high-pitched nature of her amusement drowned my warning throat clearings and told his groping fingers nothing and I saw there the colonial emblem of the islands—white man rampant on black girl suppliant. Gaden, I wonder, did you ever. . . ?

Three days of this. The amusing stories of the refugees from Club Med provided the only relief. I achieved morning four.

When I came back from the beach to the *bure* glued down by heat behind the coconut palms, I found Seb etc. etc.

Who can really blame him? How did Mr. Gaden Lockyer

behave when visiting outposts of the electorate? Did Betsy worry or was she entirely relieved by the thought that he might be making someone else pregnant? Places can breed desperation and I have an afflicting vision of my fourteen-year-old self cavorting before Mr. Renouf's rheumy eyes on the lawn in front of Villa Marina. Yet though I mentally gave Seb absolution, unfairly I used his behavior as a surface excuse for doing what I had considered doing for the last two years.

Out.

Out beyond the circumference.

I was on a home-bound plane before Seb could even blink and begin worrying about the possibility of gonorrhea, or worse, and in a rush of whipped-up outrage, had packed all my possessions into three suitcases and driven off to a Villa Marina clone somewhere in Red Hill.

As I struggled to make myself feel wounded instead of freed, I combed the jobs columns, wrote letters of application, made phone appointments for interviews. It was easier than I could have believed to transfer my minimal talents to a newspaper library where my archival skills were an asset. Graciously, private enterprise gave me three days' grace before I had to take up my position and I spent them driving up to visit mother's leaning shack.

Clarity of intent foundered as I pulled into the drive that was gradually roughing itself out in front of the house. The place was rocking with walloper music and, without even seeing, I recognized Aunt Marie's limited pianistic gambols and mother whacking away on drums as if the sticks had never been out of her hands.

I am about to present her with father's late-remembered gift.

How does Stanley like the racket one valley away?

Why was I worried about mother?

Why think she needed me? I'm the one in need.

The two old girls were radiant when I edged through the door and didn't even miss a beat as they waved one-handed welcomes. The piano, I observed in passing on my way to brew tea, was a beat-up Lipp with two ivories missing. Bonnie had moved up technologically from woodstove to primus, but even that took so long I dragged a bottle of brandy from my bag, a gift I had brought along for her, and poured myself a double. I also took out the leather drumstick case and placed it on the table beside the brandy bottle where she couldn't fail to see it.

The two of them crashed into the tonic chord. Whump whump a whumpeta whump.

Kisses hugs cries. More glasses, more pourings, and

"What's this, darling?" Bonnie asked me, picking up the cylinder and opening the flap. "What's—"

I should have done it more gently.

Her heart must have given a terrific flutter for she turned a sickening white and groped for a chair.

"Where did you get these?" she asked.

"Dad," I said.

VI

◇

I have to admit Seb made little effort to draw me back even though it gnaws my self-esteem to admit this. A few angry phone calls, one glitteringly rational letter setting out the reasons for my recanting (reasons which were, *au fond,* sordidly financial) and after that, silence.

Loneliness bothers me. I'm a natural yacker. *God,* Seb would complain, *you talk to anybody.* It's true. I talk to old ladies at bus stops, waitresses, plumbers, delivery men, shop assistants, fellow travelers on planes and trains and even diners at adjacent tables if I can. The only people I am unable to talk to, although I feel it incumbent on me to try, are doctors and psychiatrists who feel their time is worth money. Even when you pay, they still feel it isn't enough.

Yet, yet . . . after a month or so in a fusty boardinghouse from where, in bishop's swoop, I move to a bed-sitter near the river at New Farm, and after several giggle sessions with female colleagues in the newspaper morgue, I discover that I barely think of Seb, that the absence of his sporadic and selfish sexual attention was a fresh argument for celibacy and that I delight in the obligationless nature of my new domesticity. One egg or none? Shall I gulp my wedge of cheese and biscuit standing up at the kitchen counter or slumped before the telly? Eat in or out? Bliss.

Happiness is the ruined chop with no recriminatory comments.

There is time, too, for my obsessions. In the non-rarefied air of morning newspaper demands they normally have little time to flourish but I gain a reputation for industry as I appear early or stay late to pursue my own manic itch.

I make discoveries.

Mr. Gaden Lockyer, not to put too fine a point on it, was a crook. A political crook—which has a respectability this country has learned to tolerate. Now occupying an entire wall in my small flat, he watches me as I sift through take-home notes sufficient in volume to nourish the most spurious of doctoral theses. The newspaper files to which I have access contain information on public figures that pre- and post-date the year Queensland achieved autonomy. I take refreshing plunges into the deeps of the decades before and after separation even though those years hold little that is pertinent to the nub of my search. Moving forward, further unknown morsels on Gaden Lockyer surface. He had mining interests in a failed operation near Chillagoe which, taken over by a new company, was sold to the government. Mr. Lockyer and a Cabinet Colleague had pecuniary interests in the transaction. A Royal Commission was mooted. Take this: here's a studio photograph of Mackay worthies, circa 1919, sweating in their best dark suits in the non-air-conditioned fanless council chambers. It is a blueprint for all the pompous machismo of town halls and parliamentary side-rooms of the period.

I gloat. Mr. Lockyer has developed a horrible importance along with a goatee. I can hardly trace the once-amused quirk to the lips. I am tracking his career with accuracy. But what of the man?

On the surface, believe me, I am quite normal. I am punctual, efficient, polite to everyone but

"She's kind of abstracted," I overhear. " 'Distanced.' Is that the word?"

In the cubicle shelter of the washroom, I hear one cadet reporter say to the editor of the women's section as they reconstruct their faces. "She's up herself."

That's one view of it.

I live modestly within my means making no demands on Seb. I visit mother, and now Aunt Marie, dutifully every few months. Seb has long since ceased to make even shadow-play on the screen of my interest. Sometimes, but not often, I accept invitations to race meetings or Gold Coast barbecues by youthful reporters whose interest in me wanes as I fail to respond to their front-seat grapplings.

Word gets around.

I write to father in New York.

He doesn't reply.

I write again. He sends me a three-line card.

If I want male companionship it will have to be drawn from beyond the work-walls. But by now, six months after the marital schism, I am so concerned with Mr. Lockyer, who does, I admit, accompany me spiritually to concerts, theater, restaurants and sometimes in the car as far as Bonnie's hideout (he's really at his relaxed best in the country, stalking off from family whoopee on piano and drums) that I have little need for anyone else. I still talk to old ladies at bus stops, waitresses, plumbers, delivery men and even diners at adjacent booths.

I am a suitable case for treatment.

Mind you, *I* don't believe that but others would.

I have drawn a map.

I have plotted a course.

I intend plugging in to that map, under landscape, under time, swimming with my researcher's easy freestyle stroke until I surface, gasping, clutching my long-dead beau by the arm.

The morning I pack the trunk of my car at the beginning of a month's annual leave, the car radio is belting out "Sentimental Journey."

Would you believe this?

I'm a sucker for omens.

For a long time I had debated with myself the notional purity of train travel as opposed to car—it should be train to clamber into the spirit of the business—but some of the townlets, or their ghosts upon my map, are unreachable by public transport and I have no bullock driver's license. A month would be scarcely long enough though I have a flowering consciencelessness about the nature of my annual leave: rubber time, as they say in Malaysia. *Jam karet*. Rubber time.

I skirt Gungee on my way north, perhaps because Bonnie and Marie have gone public again and have a weekend engagement at a cowdown hoedown in the valleys there, and to the harmonics of "Chattanooga Choo-choo" I drive into Saturday noontime and head for Gin Gin where Boobs McAvoy, classmate of '72 and an ardent exponent of "The Rustle of Spring," has settled down with her itinerant pineapple picker. I ring from a town callbox, depending on the element of surprise for hospitality and later, welcome achieved, discover as I stand at the bottom of her veranda steps that we barely recognize each other for those first few flashing seconds, searching underyear for the face behind the present.

"Belle!" Boobs shrieks between little joy sobs. "Oh God, Belle!"

"*Dah* dah de *dah* dah, de *dah* dah!" I sing for her, my "Rustle of Spring" monstrously parodied, and she hugs me to her breasty laughter and drags me inside.

Is it too early for a drink? I wonder.

"It's never too early," Boobs says, anticipating me and choking vermouth with ice. Small nets of capillary veins on Boobs' jolly cheeks are explained.

We sit and sip and look at each other.

Her face is resuming the expected contours that once confronted me in dormitory, across the tennis net, two rows away in class, in the washroom at Slagheap railway station, surfacing, as I hope mine is.

Age, I moan inwardly. Age. If time past is irrelevant, surely Mr. Lockyer's lost decades will become void. The flash-ins! Suddenly I glimpse Clarence Renouf, Rose Burgoyne and Gaden Lockyer in three age-differentiated portraits; and the discordance of memory flings up quick snapshots of all of them—and us—tottering and aggressive, ten degrees from the vertical, cross, sour and rotting in condominiums or boardinghouses or retirement homes.

"Oh Boobs," I cry, "where's the time gone? Where's it gone to?"

Even as I lament, I suppose, my antennae are locating the manifestations of Boobs' worldly success. I know it doesn't mean happiness but nothing explains the speedy refills of vermouth. The house has a suffocatingly relaxed air culled from magazine gloss. The bottom-dented sofas are of leather. The cane loungers are upholstered in impractical white linen. Floors are polished wood of a sheen so dazzling I can see the reflection of my inelegantly crossed legs. The large and rambling house has the ability to shrink a guest and to sustain the impact of scattered expensive toys without minimizing space. From the garden comes the chatter of sprinklers tossing water on leaves. I tell her the place is lovely and she agrees with a complacency I find infuriating.

When Boobs asks me where I am heading, I am vague and indirect. She never did have an ear for the abstract. Nor an eye. Euclid routed her. But I confess to a broken marriage whose tiny island is almost submerged by the waves of months washing over that sharpest coral.

"Eight years," Boobs says. Maybe her chest has something to do with lasting the distance but another glance at her mouth informs me that time doesn't measure success. There's an edge of boredom and I remember the last occasion we met on that racketing rail-motor and I had asked her what she had in common with her pineapple picker. "Everything," silly Boobs had said.

How the splendor of this—this—estate?

"A wealthy aunt," she tells me. "Mine. Who died."

We find, after an hour, that dormitory and playing-field gossip has dried up. If my bosom companion of earlier days is troubled by possessions and regrets, she no longer finds me her confidential center. I stand on the farewelling veranda having rejected offers of lunch, dinner, the overnight stay, moved doubtless by a tiny nagging jealousy of Mr. Itinerant who has managed to entrap and successfully subdue what had always been pure ebullience, and admire the vast green acres stretching like shagpile to the purple hill-line. Inwardly the worm of search is urging me on. All Boobs has been left with is the despair of lushness.

"As far as you can see," she says, interpreting my eye and waving modestly at horizons. "It gives you a good feeling, a feeling of security, if you know what I mean."

I don't know at all what she means, except for the hopes I am pinning on my search for Gaden Lockyer.

"Something has to," I reply unkindly and instantly rue my words for her mouth wavers on admission and then shuts tight.

I am distressed for both of us. Disperse, scatter, divest. Could this mean discarding even the center?

Our final embrace has less enthusiasm. Does she detect my discoveries?

I let in the clutch and see Boobs through my rear vision mirror, for one reverse image moment shrunken to a teen-age kid in a skimpy tunic quaffing the temporariness of worldly possessions through the pores of her disillusioned skin.

The afternoon absorbs me as I drive through my mental and actual map to a town where I may hole up for the night like any general to consider strategy. A diversion is called for a sideways—knight's gambit—excursion to Mr. Lockyer's childhood farm near Hornet Bank, a chilling atrocity site where for once the native owners of the land turned the table on white invaders. Gaden's daddy, so my nit-picking research had revealed, had been an active member of punitive expeditions. How had that affected the small boy watching his father ride off to shoot black men like crows? Official biography of Mr. Lockyer senior had obliterated this piece of information that I discovered only by nosing through the preserved letters of settlers on the Upper Dawson.

I must stand by those wind-whistled walls of rotting log and slab and sniff out the earliest presence of the child before his family moved to the Condamine.

This side trip, my mind and petrol tank tell me, is folly.

Must I do this?

What are relationships between men and women intended to be?

My view of Boobs has unsettled me. What does society really want?

My mind wanders as I drive. On my zoom return from visiting my own lost daddy, I was waiting in La Guardia for my flight to Los Angeles watching another wilting pair of travelers weaving their own enclosed space. They were young but not too young. Late twenties. I related to that. I looked up from dropping a chocolate wrapper in a bin to surprise them in an eye-dive with each other that was embarrassing in its depth. I say embarrassing but then, somehow, it became comforting in its exposure of tenderness. It was genuine, wasn't it, if only for that half minute? It hit the center didn't it, if only for one second? Like Huck's sudden smile in the all-night diner or the feel of my mouth on his cheek? One moment of sincerity can pose itself proudly beside years of hypocrisy and gain grace.

The two. She was mousy, drab. Her skirt was an impossible muddy blue and too long. Her shoes were flat, and brown. The cardigan that looked home-knitted (Bonnie, you would have loved it) was in synthetic lavender fiber, cable stitch. Her eyes clung the longer. Oh how they clung! He was patting her hand, tender at this point of departure, and when I saw this I had to look away. It was hard to look away. When I dared return my eyes to them, and they were still oblivious of me, his patting paw had removed itself from hers and now rested on and encircled his other wrist which he held with such heartbreaking tenderness I feared for that drab skirt and cardigan. He had a gently tortured face, like my father's I kept thinking, a face that would move women to excesses of sentiment.

When the call came to board, the young woman walked ahead of me and took a seat in front of mine in a silence more lavender than her cable-stitch. She was to be spared nothing for immediately an overfleshed poncho wearer, breathy and wheezing, slid into the seat beside her, snuffled wetly and belched. "Oh pardon me," he begged the air. He sang quietly, as if in cynical self-parody, "Oh pardon me, pardon me." I could see by the utter stillness of the young woman's head that, while I cringed from the antisocial noises, she had not even glanced in his direction, so impaled was she on her central point of love and departure. Poncho reached up and pressed the call button. "May I have some Kleenex?" he asked the hostess softly and winningly. "I have this very heavy cold." He proved he had this heavy cold and the hostess drew herself fastidiously backwards and went off to the galley. When she returned she handed him the tissues with a fully extended arm making its criticism plain and I could have laughed at that and even at the revolting sound of nasal clearing that followed were it not for the unmoving wounded posture of the woman at his side. He acted as if the seat next to him were vacant. I guess it was if we accept that physical presence means nothing in the absence of the spirit. Poncho spoke to himself, soothingly. She did not stir. He began humming, humming and talking alternately, ignoring the meals placed before him, the withdrawn body at his side.

After we touched down at Los Angeles he swung away into space at the terminal with the frightening lightness, the weightlessness, of fat men that has its own menace while Blue Skirt, cumbered by her very lack of weight, lugged her bag with an effort over to the schedule screen and began peering astigmatically. I longed to speak, to comfort, to say anything at all.

What could I say?

◇ ◇ ◇

Relationships! Yeah!

Here's another on my way to the center.

Ten years have passed since I last saw Mr. Bonsey, schoolyard spunk who propositioned me between play lunch at eleven and the midday recess. Even before I had moved on he had applied for an up-country teaching post, to be dutifully but unwillingly close to aged parents. As far as I know he is still there. I will smoke him out without warning in his small school near Hornet Bank, my visit a kind of social appetizer before the main course of my travel takes over. After all, this is my area, the outer periphery of Drenchings and Jericho Flats.

I time my arrival to coincide with the last bell of the afternoon, dawdling along unsurfaced back roads until I arrive at the township of Taroom where I drink a fly-spotted cup of tea in an ancient milkbar and munch time. I have checked into the town's better hotel and feel a certain confidence mingle with my curiosity as I drive, bristling with directions, out beyond the school to inspect what time has done to Mr. Bonsey.

Never go back, people say. Never.

Where is the handsome roué who glided around the schoolyard above Moreton Bay confident of conquest? Poor Mr. Bonsey has suffered a stroke of some magnitude and one eye, the glad eye, is half closed. This makes him look sinister, untrustworthy—unfairly, I suppose, for one always knew exactly where one stood with Mr. Bonsey. His left hand is hooked into a useless arc from temporary paralysis though he assures me physiotherapy has made it functional once more.

He is almost unrecognizable.

In the family home, a puzzle box of overfurnished rooms, he sags on a divan clutching a scotch. I clutch another. Where are the aged parents, I wonder. Bitterly he tells me they have gone to retirement homes.

"Separate retirement homes," he explains sourly. "After fifty years of marriage they split up in the end, can you believe it? Can't bear the sight or sound of each other."

I want to laugh and stifle it. "Fifty years," Mr. Bonsey says angrily. "She must have laundered eight thousand shirts in that time and that's just for starters and then the old bastard sneaks off to a friendly doctor who hides him away fast in a nursing home where she can't get at him. His words. So what can the old girl do except find another? I couldn't cope, what with this stroke and all. God!" he says savagely. "What a life! That's marriage for you."

He limps over to the fridge to get more ice. The house is untidy, dark, comfortless. It's nightmare country. Through an open side door I can see his dying garden, shrubs keeling over from lack of water. A truck hurtles past on the main road and the dust seeps over the plants and into the sitting room.

"I was married," I confess. "I understand how they must have felt."

He's not interested in me. He doesn't seem to have heard.

"I finally gave in," he said. "Married, I mean. Pretty girl. Pretty as paint. I thought when I saw her I've got to get into bed with that but she went for the formal bit. That should have warned me. So there I was tied up, ready to give her everything and two years after I brought her home here I had this damn stroke and when I got out of hospital she'd gone. Deserting me in my hour of need, the bitch. What do you think of that, eh?"

I don't think anything much. I'm beginning to understand expediency. Somehow, looking around the house, looking at Mr. Bonsey, a vanished charmer, and thinking of his aged gum-munching parents, I sympathize with her. I doubt if I would have lasted a week. But he is working away at his wound, determined to inflame it. "Would you desert someone when they needed you?" he persisted. His one good eye gives a hopeful flash of the old boulevardier.

"Needed me for what?" I temporize.

"Of course you wouldn't. My God, am I going to shaft that bitch! She's after half of everything. More than half. House, car, the lot. I'll give her half! God, she wouldn't even sleep with me for the last year, I ask you."

Don't ask me, I think. There is a new coarseness about Mr. Bonsey that I could not recall his displaying in the old days. He tells an off-color joke. He fails to register my po-faced reaction.

"Couldn't sit out the stroke. Too much to ask. I've had to do everything for myself. Every goddamn thing." Gloomily he tops up his drink and forgets about mine. "Anyway, she was being laid by the town clerk, for God's sake. The bitch. Just because I had a temporary setback. God, I had an erection this morning." He mentions it wistfully as if it's an old friend he hasn't seen for a very long time. "Don't know why. Must have known you were coming."

This is terrible.

"It just means you're getting better," I say.

He staggers back to his couch and collapses against a stack of cushions. "Forgive me," he says, "for lying down like this. A day in class and I've had it."

The truck returns and more dust drifts onto the floor, the furniture, his words. One could be buried alive. I want to leave. I can't bear him or the room.

"Don't you think," I suggest, groping for openings, "it would be better if you moved, applied for a transfer, something. This house is too big for you. You must get worried about intruders."

I bend down to retrieve my glass from the floor where I have placed it and on looking up find I am gazing straight into the barrel of a shotgun he has whipped out from under the divan covers. It is pointed directly at my face from six feet and, behind his trigger finger, there's a wild smile.

"I'm safe enough," he says. "There are guns all over."

He's mad, I decide. Crazy.

There's been no laughing discussion of the old days at the bay. No interest in me. Not one question about my lifestyle or work. No guffaws over Mrs. Burgoyne. He is so absorbed in self, he is his own center, the ultimate Euclidean point nurturing nothing but his own lopped pride.

Although he had laid down the gun my bladder distresses me.

I ask for the bathroom and there find a rifle leaning matily beside the toilet bowl. I wet myself. I glance into a bedroom as I pass and there's another gun lying on the bed.

"I have to go now," I tell Mr. Bonsey when I return to the living room. "Have to hit the road."

"The bitch," he says. "See that greenhouse out the back? See that? Prize orchids. Can't be bothered now." He points to a couple of tacky felt ribbons dangling above the mantelpiece. "Won prizes for them. Look, I had everything going for me. God, I'll shaft her."

Enough.

I pick up my tote bag. I walk firmly to the door.

"It's getting late," I lie. "I have to be in Drenchings tonight."

He doesn't hear.

"We're the ones. We should have got together," he suggests hopefully as I reach the top of the steps. He hasn't used my name once, I notice. Maybe he has forgotten it. He is limping after me, still holding his scotch.

"Goodbye," I say, offering my hand, programmed for politeness.

He ignores it.

Irrelevantly he begins another blue story as if we are guests at a party.

"Take care," I suggest, halfway down the steps, and I hear him say, "Write to me, will you?"

Before I have even engaged the motor he has gone inside again to the dying furniture, the unswept floor, the pileup of food dishes and the guns.

I drive beyond the fences of his tomb, go back to the hotel, cancel my room and drive into my own obsession.

Already.

I am driving into cardboard.

Let me tell you how.

I can hardly believe I have achieved this.

It's a blow-up of Gaden Lockyer complete with wife and children outside his slab farmhouse in the Upper Burdekin. The blow-up is twelve feet by eight and everyone is life-size. It's hard to reconcile this with its archival print original six inches by four.

"I want to fit that woman," I had explained badly to the man in the camera shop. Maybe I am no better than Mr. Bonsey.

"You what?"

I don't blame him. Lately I have become awkward with words as explanatory devices. I could hardly summarize my intentions publicly. But the shop, he assured me, would make posters any size: Red Square size, friends of the people size, any size within reason. The cost would be even bigger.

"It's for a feature wall," I lied. No. That wasn't a lie. There was nowhere else to put it. It took up, smothered, the entire end wall of my bed-sitter. My obsession was assuming a new slant. I ordered two of them and the man in the shop had looked slantwise into my calm demented eyes, pursed his lips and looked down.

The posters are ready two or three months before I begin my journey backwards. Let me go back at least those few months.

I lie there on my sleepless bed and watch Mr. Lockyer grimly holding his peeing child and half-smiling half-grimacing across its bawling head at Mrs. Lockyer who stands in a flurry of wood shavings no one has bothered to sweep up yet. Her dark hair is pulled back rather prettily into a loose bun and imaginative wisps drop across her forehead. She's too tired to smile back and her eyes are weepy (I wish I knew their color) and she wears what seems to be a patterned blouse tucked into the full and tight-waisted skirts of those times. There are three children older than the baby and the house isn't even finished. I can see sky through a bush-pole annexe erected to one side of the main shack. You poor bitch, I think. Poor poor bitch.

I get up from the bed and stand in front of her. Allowing for the difference between my floor level and hers, she is exactly my height. The enlarger has seen to that. My hair is pulled back like hers and I think, looking into the mirror

I have placed strategically on the opposite wall, that we really are rather alike. Especially with the hat. I forgot to mention the hat, a floppy straw arrangement with two ribbons dangling at her nape. It took me weeks to find that hat and I finally had to steal it from the props department of a theater company which was doing a period piece last summer. I wish I knew if the color was right. I settled for that battered straw yellow.

I turn, revolving demurely, watching myself from my sideways eyes and smile back at Gaden. (I have begun to use his first name.) His wife is obliterated.

So while I smile, I remove my housecoat which I too have worn tightly belted, and stand naked for him, naked bar my shoes whose heel height brings me level with Betsy. Does his smile shift slightly?

Here I am peering intently at our reflected images and the baby's howling is driving me mad and young Aubrey (I know the name's right—it took me a week of checking at the central registrar of births) has just kicked dust and woodchips at Liz's clean white pinafore I starched specially for this photograph. Her young sister is starting to cry. But I smile and keep smiling and reach across and try to take Gaden's paper hand.

I have to watch this. I must be careful.

Only last week I very nearly made holes in the poster's backing trying to dig my fingers into his arm.

I am looking for the right clothing, I tell him. *Forgive my nakedness* (hoping he'll whisper, It's my pleasure), *standing here in my dewy skin.* There's a dressmaker in Valley Junction who is working on a skirt and blouse for me. She thinks it's the coming length or that I'm needing fancy dress for the theater company I stole from. I tell her conflicting lies. But when I try on the skirt with a pair of button-up boots

I've also filched from a heritage museum in South Brisbane, she begins to wonder.

I am assembling myself.

I am getting into the right frame.

Of mind.

I don't think the project is affecting my work, though my colleagues, when they bother to speak to me these days, tell me outright that I am becoming distracted, unmindful, and had better sharpen up. Once last month the chief sub bawled me out when I forgot to send up the material he asked for. Actually he more than bawled. He threatened with "One more balls-up like this, miss, and you're out." I rather liked him. He's a small intense man with violet eyes and he wears an eyeshade. They say it's no affectation but a visual weakness that makes him peculiarly allergic to fluorescent lighting. I believe this. Sometimes when I have allowed Mr. Lockyer to slip from my awareness for an hour or so (yes, it is as intense as this), I could almost wish the chief sub would take my hand. It might help but it's unlikely that we could ever play sweaty palms. He's a crusty thirty-and-more years ahead of me and is still happily married to the cadet reporter he met in Sydney four decades ago. They are welded by grandchildren and even if he did take my hand, lingering over a proffered sheaf of clippings, it would be merely to pat it aside. Fatherly.

So I live with a paper lover. There was a corny song during the second world war the words of which went something like *I'm gunna buy a paper doll that I can call my own, a doll that other fellas cannot steal.* Bonnie and Marie used to beat it out for dances. I think of this. My emotional itch is absurd. Crass. Some might even say perverted, obscene. But how pleasant to wake in subtropic summer and find his gaze two degrees to my right, a gaze that will settle on me when I press myself into that lost moment of his life northwest of Hornet Bank.

Despite making no direct inquiries about Seb, acquaintances I run into on the Queen Street Mall tell me he has taken Patch over from Frank Hassler. I could have foreseen this. What I could not have foreseen is that Patch would leave him within months for a handsome lady real estate agent with prospects who was cutting a swathe through the Gold Coast with Japanese clients. An enraged Seb was talking high-pitchedly of dykes, lumping me in with them to the morbid delight of these sexual scroungers who would watch as they told for the giveaway flicker.

How titillated they would be to know my neurosis is less satisfyingly fleshly and a world more crazed.

Maybe I have been wrong all along and am a center looking for a circumference. A Pirandellian problem.

As if the car objects to the vibrations of landscape as I drive closer to Hornet Bank, it judders and runs itself to a halt miles from anywhere. Is it a technical or a psychic pause? I check petrol, water, oil. All correct. Battery? Spark plugs? Fan belt? Transmission? Fuel line? God love me, I don't know. How do I gauge dust and grit in the arteries of my car? The gravel road on which I am marooned winds off to the west between strangely empty paddocks whose tree borders crowd in on me unmoving. Something insists that I should, at this point, whether I like it or not, be traveling by horse and sulky. It is as if the countryside rejects the alien character of my mode of transport and, more that that, as if it rejects my color, my language, my personal search. It threatens. The stillness of the scrub, the lack of insect hum, are menacing.

I will give myself, I say, fifteen minutes and not a second more for a car to pass and if nothing turns up start walking for the nearest farm.

It does not resemble farming country. Miles of tea-tree scrub and gidgee stretch away to north and south and though the road is used, its surface has a pondering air of infrequency. I wait and wait. I hum right through a Bach prelude. I wait. Grass at the road edge hangs rangily limp through the broken fenceline. The trees could be painted drop-scenes.

No one comes.

But I sense the landscape moving in as I sit in the driver's seat, the prelude finished and smoking what I intend as a nonchalant cigarette, tapping one foot, occasionally trying to start the engine which barks and dies. The landscape shambles in as the afternoon closes downward, pincering me too close to that massacre thirteen decades away. Where were you, Gaden, that jittering morning? Were you slopping oatmeal on your bib thirty miles off?

Panicked, I am out of the car in a door-banging rush and striding west into paper shadows, mile after mile. This is a pocket where no birds sing. Our country is full of them, spirit circles that reject intruders. Yet after an hour a thinning in the trees near a road-fork that will take me out in the general direction of Drenchings reveals pasture and sorghum sweeps and slow home-wending cows on hillslopes. My spirits rise to meet the ridgecap of a distant galvanized roof.

All the way up the home-track to the house, the desolation of the place appals. A truck carcass rusts beneath pepper trees and under the shadows of sprawling figs the homestead crouches shabbily on the brow of the rise, smoke lazing up from a kitchen lean-to. My progress is attended by barking as a snapping blue heeler heads like a ferret from a side shed and races toward me, ripping at air. Somewhere behind, a man moves center stage to stand watching as I cope with yelps and teeth, watching just that back-country shade too long as the dog corners me, before he decides to call cut with a whistle. The heeler retreats, loathing me, and props, panting and dribbling. Self-consciously, the dog working closely at my heels, I jerk up the track between cowpats to the ancient shape on the veranda.

It is not so aged. Sun, wind, dry seasons have plowed the landscape of his face into infertile furrows. His features emerge from the shadow of his hat and he waits, head back, for me to speak first. Out of exhaustion. My exhaustion. The bastard, I think. Where's that vaunted bush friendliness? I'm sweaty and dust-streaked. I make apologetic sounds. I tell him about the car. He lets me tell him. I ask if there's a telephone and he nods eastward. "Another few miles," he replies, without malice, but without much interest. "The people at Eurombah have one of them things."

I start to cry and his face goes awkward.

"Want a cuppa?" he asks and answers himself directly. "Stupid question, eh? The missus is just boiling up."

The kitchen is painted with the smoke-stains of decades through which the wood stove glints in the dusk while the missus, a chunky incurious woman, nods shortly in my direction and planks an extra mug down. We sit and regard each other. Under the table I edge off my joggers and rub stinging feet together. I try to mop up my face with a tissue. I don't like to mention the car again. It seems to have passed from the farmer's mind. His wife pushes a plate of brownies across and unexpectedly answers my anxiety. "Car stuck, eh? We get quite a bit of that. You're the seventh this fortnight." She munches happily.

Her husband drinks his first mug rapidly and tops it up.

"We'll take a look at it when you've had your tea," he says. "Drink up."

I tell them my name and they ask where I'm headed and when I tell them back of Drenchings the word engages the woman's interest.

"Got family that way," she says. "Still up there."

I tell her that once I had too and by the time I have established my identity and we've swapped a few local names, she checks my own name again and I realize I've given her my father's. When I re-identify with my grandparents, her whole face lights up with lost girlhood and in seconds she is babbling about mother and Aunt Marie as if they were the coziest of old mates. I can't believe my luck. It's a big country but there aren't many people, not here, not out in the sticks. In black-stump landscape, coincidence is the name of the game, country where farmers travel a hundred miles for provisions or lunch or even a beer and never give it a thought.

My feet have stopped throbbing and oversweetened tea is propping me up. I hesitate then decide to take a dive into candor. "I'm not going back to the old place," I admit. "Grandmother sold Perjury Plains some years back. Maybe for a look. I don't know. It all depends on the time I've got. I'm after something else. Research." Is that vague enough? The portmanteau qualities of the word dazzle me. I hope they dazzle others. "I'm heading for a place outside Drenchings. I don't even know if it's still there. A little town called Jericho Flats."

The missus utters a small squeal of recognition.

Jackpot!

She nudges her tea-swilling husband. "You hear that? The Flats? That was Lockyers' old farm," she says, swinging back to me. "Well, waddya know? That was my mother's name, love. Lockyer." (Are we proxily related?) "She came from over the hills a piece, out past Cockatoo. Moved out to the coast a few years back, just before she died. Said she needed a breath of salt air after all the bulldust. We all do."

I have passed beyond disbelief in happenchance and am immersed in the spangled irrationality of predoomed occasions. My car stopped for a reason. There's no incredible coincidence in this, not in this country with figures scattered over thousands of square miles, figures who have hung in there fighting landscape through heroic and dying generations. My body forgets fatigue as I press, delicately, for information. There was a brother, she tells me, her uncle, still living at the old place. She'd ring if only they had a phone. "What is it you're after exactly?"

I tell her I work for a newspaper library which has asked me to unearth material for a series of articles they plan on the earliest settlers in these parts. Her face has resumed a doubting, faintly suspicious look. I keep stressing the word research. It has an impersonal tone, an academic flavor. It has weight. I assure her that I am not a reporter. "Researcher," I repeat, smoothing the long vowels over her. Her husband had long since lost interest in his wife's crackpot relatives and is brewing more tea.

"Fresh lot," he offers as if the excitement of nascent acquaintance wasn't taking place.

"Mind you," the missus warns, "uncle's getting on a bit. Must be well over seventy by now. We only get to see him a couple of times a year, specially round Christmas when we have a bit of a get-together, see? Stuck out there on his own outside the Flats. We always drop over with a chook, just to cheer the old bugger up. A chook and a bottle of brandy. That's what he likes. Not that he needs that much cheering, mind. He's not short of a dollar. He's sold off most of the place and rolls in and out between the Flats and the pub at Drenchings. He can tell you a mint about the old days. If you miss him out at the house, he'll be in at the pub. That's where he'll be."

Let us skip one hour. Two. My car is towed back to the farm by this slow-moving husband who, head under the hood, a flashlight propped by the side of the car, performs a minor miracle to the fuel line by sucking on it and spitting out gobfuls of clotted seed and dust. They wave me off in the dark filled with tea and messages for the old bugger, and I drive and drive until I find Drenchings snoozing beside its river junction, unchanged in my absence, its pub languid with evening.

It's late and the town is still, not even the fading raucousness of closing-time drinkers spilling into the night. From one of the old houses across the road from the pub, a house I still remember, floats a fragment of Victoriana as someone behind that shrunken timber plays an Albéniz tango on guitar, a hesitant searching plucking of molten notes that drift moonwards. I wait, parked, unwilling to enter the hotel until the moment is over, trapped in the rending antithesis of this scrubber township with its deserted main street, closed shops and silent pub and the air vibrating with haunting perfection as notes like tears throb, melt and fade into dust and white air.

Hello, old town. Hello. I've been waiting a long time for this.

In the penulimate year of wedlock breakdown—I hesitate to call it "marriage"—Seb had taken to jogging and wore that cliché of a T-shirt inscribed *New York Paris London Dirranbandi*. It was still a novelty then and he met a lot of people that way. "Hey!" they'd yell passing him on River Road or the Botanic Gardens or on the track round the university campus. "Hey! That's great!"

"It's a social comment," he would explain modestly flaunting his chest at late-night barbecues, "on the great Australian loneliness. It's anti-cringe. It's a people-meeter."

(Seb, you were a people-eater. I'm the one. Maybe I should have a shirt printed up. *San Diego New York Drenchings*. Fazer!)

Why, I ask myself, opening the door of my overnight room, are country pubs so lonely, their rooms such gasping prototypes for dreariness. Stale air wafts in gasps from each self-stuck cupboard drawer. The bed has been made and unused for months. The transom into the hall is jammed. The veranda door opens onto a twelve-foot width of unpainted planking with outcast loungers whose plastic skin is peeling. There's no joy. There is joy. Believe this. Two opposites combine in my spirit and even as I am oppressed by a decade of such rooms heaving on my shoulders, I am uplifted by the notion of Mr. Gaden Lockyer booking in here when he came into town by buggy on business. Did the old house across the road once rattle to "The Rustle of Spring?"

I lie on my lumpy bed and wish the wall facing me were obliterated by my friendly blow-up.

As I trudge the nextday streets of this township, enter and leave shops, I realize that I am being assessed as an intruder, that I cannot force myself back in time through the blink of a camera shutter in split-second exposure, but I can make use of that elasticity of time. Rubber time.

◇ ◇ ◇

Why would any seeming stranger come here is the unspoken question paramount on faces that deal with my breakfast eggs, my purchase of film, my tentative requests for directions. The town is contained, is its own center and resents outsiders. But my feet are making time-prints on those of Mr. Lockyer and eventually, eventually, I drive out beyond the sad storefronts and follow one, two, three sets of muddled directions until a twenty-mile branch road of stubborn gravel leads me to the broken gate and worn truckruts of Lockyers' farm. The little township has long gone.

Uncle, the poor old bugger, is out by the trash heap in a nimbus of flies, a stringy-bark ancient in flannel shirt, old army issue trousers and a stained felt bush hat pulled low against the sun. The moment my feet crunch round the side of the house he looks up and glares.

"Thought it'd be you."

My heart stops.

"Why?" Smiles won't work here.

"They were talking at the pub last night. Said you were coming."

Who said? Who? Bush telegraph is its own miracle.

I nod. He grumbles, "They said you were digging into the family background." His dimming eyes challenge mine for a moment.

I decide to counter his challenge with skilled lies.

With the pre-programmed approach of an encyclopaedia salesman I side-step his opener by giving my family name. "And not quite," I say. " 'Digging' is not the right word. Not family background, local history." I repeat the phrase.

"Your grandfather was a man of importance in these parts. More than that."

The lies fly easily past my teeth while the old man grunts and pokes at his rubbish fire with a bit of stick. Finally he concedes a fragment of grin.

"You've got a cheek," he says. "What's it all for, eh? Some paper they said. Bloody nosers. Don't want no reporters nosing around."

"I'm not a reporter," I tell him patiently. "I'm a library assistant who just happens to be working in a newspaper library. There is a difference." I wait for him to absorb this. As I wait his eyes wander back down the track to my parked car, an unfortunate flashy red. I follow his eyes and bumble on with words that jazz around him with the flies: ". . . preparing a series of articles . . . folk who opened up this part of the country . . . pioneers . . . Lockyer family's contribution." His eyes flicker with something close to disbelief. "And not only your grandfather. He was chosen because he was also a state Member. I've several other families to interview round Rockhampton and Mackay. People on cane farms. It's all aboveboard. No family skeletons. The paper wants to pay them tribute, that's all. Unsung heroes."

He grunts, non-committal. "Who you want to know about?"

"Your grandfather, mainly."

He looks up at me slyly. "Can't remember much about him," he says. "Only when I was a nipper. He gave me a bike one Christmas. That's mainly what I recall. Not much, eh?"

His lack of memory gives him a sense of triumph. The flies from the outback privy are going crazy about us, despite the smoke from the trash heap. I wonder how to suggest going indoors but he solves it for me.

"Better come on up. Get outa this damn sun."

Flies are busy in the house as well. His mind is still worrying around, still suspicious I can tell, as he sets the tea things down.

"You not writing a book, are you?"

"No. I told you. I'm a research librarian."

Maybe he's deaf. Maybe he's just old. Maybe he's a picker.

"A what?"

I explain as simply as I can. I repeat my name. I go back to the car, braving the flies, and fetch up a boiled fruitcake his niece has sent which seems to placate him and establish my identity finally, for a note falls out from the tea-cloth the cake is wrapped in and I watch him read it and then put the bit of paper up on a shelf. I decide not to mention the word newspaper again. I hope he's forgotten it.

"It's a big project," I say vaguely. "We're looking for old photographs, old letters and diaries, shopping lists, anything that might give information about life-styles in those days. We want to store it so that, well, so that historians can make use of it."

I have decided to omit further reference to the printed word.

"Can't see the point of it, eh."

I try looking sweet. I smile a lot. "We're after the really important things like the time your grandfather was elected to Parliament. The time of that mining boom outside Drenchings. The two big floods late last century. We want to know what your grandfather did for the people of his electorate. That sort of thing."

"Sugar?" He shoves over a lumpy bowl. "He never did much for us out here that I know about. Them politician fellers are all the same, in it for what they can get out of it. Milk?"

"Thank you," I say. "This is very kind."

He despises me for that. "Not kind. You must have forgot. Bush practice, eh."

"I know," I say humbly. "I do know. My own folk came from farther out."

"Heard that," he says. "Someone said something at the pub. Anyway, me niece wrote, like you saw."

He regards me with his head on one side like an old rooster.

"So you're Bonnie's girl, eh? I knew your mum when she was knee-high to a grasshopper. And later. God, that old Bonnie! Well, she wasn't that old last I saw her. Could she tickle a pianner! Bon's girl, turned detective like." (He expects a laugh for that one. I give it.) "And there was a sister, too, wasn't there? Bon's that is. Your grandpa never had no boys. No, don't tell me. Let me nut it out. She was the older one, wasn't she? Marcia. No, wait a mo. That's not it. Marie. It was Marie, wasn't it?"

"That's right," I say. "My aunt." He gives me a doggy grin and I build up his goodwill by telling him about the family while he chips in with a question here and there and says, "Jesus Christ, it's all coming back. It's all coming back."

As we tail each other crossing the barriers, things become repetitious. How much is reality, how much fantasy?

"Went courtin your mum," he confesses with a sideways look, "when she was grown up a bit. But I was too old for her. Guess she never even noticed and then she went off and got herself tied up with some Yank. I lost touch after that. Only saw her folks once in a while. Lovely girl though. And could she play that pianner!''

''Marie was the real pianist,'' I insist. ''Bonnie took up drums. They started a band. I suppose you know.''

''Course I know,'' the old man says testily. ''Danced to 'em, haven't I? Course she played drums but I remember her playing proper stuff, you know, when we had evenings at the hall in Drenchings. ''Rustle of Spring.'' Funny how I can remember that. But I do. Just like yesterday. I can still see her up on that stage, all the streamers, playing away and looking a real treat in a white dress. Fancy remembering that.''

There's a tear in that dimming eye.

Other tributaries begin flowing.

Judiciously I steer him towards my grandparents and it isn't long before I persuade a family album out of him and endure half a rambling hour of strangers with blurred faces while his commentary takes side and backwards turns until, nosing through a loose pile of snapshots, shutter memories, he pushes a yellowed rectangle of cardboard mounting under my nose and says, ''Is that what you're after?''

Spring and Fall.

''Who's the little boy?''

''Me. Course it's me. Unmistakable mug. Grandpa Lockyer and me—oh, taken maybe sixty years back. How's that, eh?''

''Marvelous!'' I tell him, hoping my hungry eyes will not reveal my mania. ''Marvelous.''

Mr. Gaden Lockyer is looking very elderly indeed in his double-breasted suit and stiff white collar. The youthful sideways tilt of his mouth has taken a deeper groove but the eyes stare back at me with interest. My pictured host, now mumbling a wedge of his niece's boiled fruitcake, is in a sailor suit and cap. His legs are encased in the long socks fashionable then. He looks as if he is terrified of the photographer.

"Oh this is wonderful! Really wonderful!" I have ceased to notice the small boy in the sailor suit. "This must have been taken only a few years before he died. Your grandfather, that is. One of the last, I suppose. You don't have any others, do you?"

The old man makes creaky noises and says something about a box of stuff in the horse shed. "Waste of time keeping all this old stuff." He tells me he was married not long after my mother went away but his wife and the baby died the next year. "Never bothered after that," he says. "Didn't seem worth it, somehow. I was gettin too old."

I think of another old man in a trailer park who kept nothing. Is this the ultimate acceptance of the dying process, this divesting of all mortal reminders, the momentary futility of our moth-cycle noted?

It is a delicate moment. The box. I hate to press an advantage at the wrong time. I have finished my own wedge of cake and a second cup of tea. I'm fulsome in my thanks but I don't want to overdo it. The box. He's still wily. I start to rise in the middle of my gratitude and ask cautiously would he care to join me for dinner in town. I will be there for one more night, I tell him. He doesn't appear to understand my invitation. Eating out? It's a city concept beyond his backwoods life-span. I try again, suggesting he join me in the hotel dining room for tea and his eyes blink their understanding and he begins a frightful aged snigger of embarrassment.

"God, missie, what'd they all say, eh? What'd they say? This is a small town. Can't afford to ruin me reputation."

Insincerely I laugh heartily with him, perfect synchronization. No semitone apart here. He still believes he's a dasher! I think of Mr. Bonsey and wince.

"You're joking, aren't you?" I suggest, still smiling round the words. "Please. Do come. You'll be doing me a great favor. I feel so awful eating alone in a strange hotel. Look, we're almost related, aren't we? I mean Bonnie would love to know you're taking care of me." I try to look younger. "She'd be tickled pink."

He turns away from me whacking his pipe out on the edge of the table. Tobacco ash falls all over the floor.

"Got no duds," he says. "No good duds, not for dining out."

"Who cares about duds," I say. "They don't in the city. And it's your town, isn't it? No one cares. We can have a drink first. You'd like that?"

He grunts some more and I can feel him slipping away. The box. My hands shuffle dozens of yellowed snaps like playing cards and I play my ace. It's a group of three, two misty young women and an older man watched by a line of gumtrees.

"There," I cry, phony inspiration, "there's one of you with mother." I hope it's mother. It won't do to peer too closely. I am not sure at all about Aunt Marie and only hope it is the younger version of this old man before me.

"Show me," he orders, taking the snap from my fingers and bringing the foggy trio up close to his eyes. Is my luck gambler's or is he merely pretending to a clarity of eyesight that has long deserted him? "By geez," he admits. "You're right. That must have been taken more than thirty years ago. Just before your mum and her sister went away. The girls came over with their folks for a bit of a bush picnic at the Flats after the show. Well, now, fancy that, eh? Fancy that.''

I am almost too busy marveling at my throw of the dice to boggle with him. I must admit that mother is barely recognizable in a flap-brimmed sunhat and I cannot afford to trip on the truth or lie of my wild hazard. He's softening. His face is mushy with sentiment as he looks at this lost laughing self, avuncular hands on the shoulders of my aunt and my not-yet mother, gathering up all the girls on a sunny day by a riverbank, cicada-loud, the embroidered edges of the lunch cloth on the grass just glimpsed by the camera. I press further claims while he is befuddled with the past, suggesting he bring along that old box from the horse shed so that I can go through it and see what I can find of mother. I am hoping that by now he has forgotten the original excuse for my visit. ''She would love to see this!'' I cry. ''Love to. She's always talking about the old days, times when she was a girl. She'd be crazy for this.'' My deceitful finger touches the old snap, gently, oh so gently. I am ashamed as he looks up tear-blearily and says, ''You reckon?''

''Oh yes. I reckon.''

Trumped.

He hedges his bets. ''If I don't turn up,'' he complains seeing me off, ''it means the old truck's had it. Bloody ol' bomb.''

I accuse him of making excuses, threaten to come and fetch him. I draw the finest of lines between gravity and flirtatiousness.

''Gawd,'' he reprimands, ''don't do that. Don't come and fetch me. The whole place'd never let me hear the end of it. Always was a bit of a Casanova, eh? Kept me safe, after the wife. Safe and free.''

I look down the hall of his empty house, his dying grounds. The air vibrates with the shallowest, the thinnest of memories. How long now has he washed up one plate one mug one pan in that lonely kitchen with a static-warped radio flickering the news of cities through his evenings and the stirring whimpers of his dog?

"You bet it has," I tell him.

A normal wall poster is about sixty inches by forty-eight.

Apart from the life-size ones I have already had made of Mr. Lockyer and family, one of which decorates the wall of my Brisbane flatette, I confess to another that is more like something seen in dictatorland—the people's square in Moscow or Beijing. It caused my friendly developer enormous trouble and me enormous cost. He thinks I am mad and perhaps he is right. It is packed in the trunk of the car, carefully folded and tight-rolled, reinforcements at each corner with holes in the reinforcements through which I have threaded lengths of twine.

I am going to enter the picture. Put myself right through and beyond it. The trick is to do it within the click of a shutter.

It is one in the morning and old Mr. Lockyer's box, dredged up from under a mound of rotting sacks and saddles behind a sulky with splintered shafts, is beginning to yield its heart. At first delve it was disappointing.

There are accounts, lists of farm needs, old copies of local newspapers, the *Queenslander,* the *Ladies' Home Journal* on whose dog-eared corners my X-ray vision detects the fingerprints of Betsy Lockyer on candle-guttering evenings. I have a tenderness gland I did not suspect. Seeing her faint pencil notations on various pages (they can only be hers. I work from the dates on the magazines) and recognizing over-worn creases at certain fashion sections, the pencil tick beside the shirtwaist or the feathered hat that her up-country heart must have lusted after, I weep. God, it is one in the morning and I am weeping in this drab hotel room, unsated by an overcooked dinner, my guest, grandson Lockyer, deposited safe by now within his own crumbling walls. I am unable to sleep, kept awake by the urgency of my curiosity and a promise to return the box in the morning. There's no time for sleep. The sifting must take place now.

There are dozens of meaningless photographs. Sometimes there is a barely decipherable penciled note on the back. There are too many formal groups of important people against studio velvet, their importance now nothing. Ah it's sad, it's sad. Some few are of Gaden Lockyer whose face in later photos has been enriched by a deep scar on the temple. These photos I purloin without a qualm. First lies, now thieving. Some riches. But there will be more. Right at the bottom of the box under a pile of school homework books whose "How I spent my holidays" and "The worst moment of my life" reveal in their round childish hands nothing of Mr. Gaden Lockyer, are several notebooks, their cheap cardboard covers moldy and split, their pages glued together by damp and despair.

I am my own stout Cortez silent upon a bed in Drenchings. Looking into Chapman's Homer will be nothing to this.

January 2nd, I read. The journal is for the year 1898.

I deliberately turn page after page until I come to the day it is now, the day of my own Darien peak, the day my present and his past converge.

There is no entry.

I turn back a page.

June 10th, I read. *I have been feeling strange all day. Betsy says it is the weather and maybe the pork we had last night which Mr. Percy sent over from his farm. I don't think so. I have this sense of waiting, of attendance. Perhaps it is because I am beginning to think we should sell up. Is something about to happen to us all or just me? Betsy and the children are calm enough. I am so excited this evening and my heart raced so much when I went out on the veranda for my evening pipe, I had to go back in and take a nip of brandy to calm me down. Tomorrow? What will there be? What is it?*

Mr. Lockyer has a firm and fading hand. I am relieved to note the fulsomeness of his sentences rather than the truncated statements one associates with diary jottings. Perhaps it is because he is using the same sort of notebooks his children used for their school assignments. Involuntarily my fingers caress the letters he has formed, lingering on a word here, a word there. I touch where he touched. The sweat would have dried out decades ago but I bend my face to sniff the paper and the whiff of humanity remains if only in the depositions of weather.

I turn the pages slowly. I am terrified it might all sound like Diary of a Nobody.

I move forward, assured I am moving into my own future.

There is silence for a week, then

June 24th. I must put this down in full. Last week has been the strangest of my life. On the Wednesday after breakfast I rode up to the far corner of the farm a mile or so away to shift some of the milkers back into the next paddock where the feed is better down by the creek. It was a perfect day, blue and yellow, enough nip in the air for these latitudes to make me whistle. (Pucker up, Gaden, I urge.) *Bluey was trotting beside the horse snapping at flies. I must get down all the details. I had no warning of what was to come. The track across the paddocks was clear. If I looked back I would see the smoke of the stove rising pencil straight above our farm roof. Then this woman. Walking straight from the grove of ironbarks towards me.*

I thought at first it was a man, she was so outlandishly dressed. Trousers and shirt like a farm boy. But as I rode closer I could see her hair pulled back in a long fair tail, so fair it was almost white and her face delicate and singularly moulded. I thought I recognised her from my visit to Brisbane last year but when I called out to her my mouth seemed emptied of sound though I could hear that she was speaking, calling Good morning. She said something about it being a long way but even though she spoke and even though I clearly heard these words, nothing moved in her face, neither her mouth nor her eyes. Her eyes which were a clear and shining grey looked through me and though I could hear her *words, mine were soundless. Here we were—her speaking though closed lips, me answering with open mouth and no words at all. 'Can I help you?' I asked. 'Can I help?' She walked straight past me down towards the cottage, right through Bluey's yapping, and I watched her body moving briskly between grass clumps, striding like a boy. Betsy had come outside to empty the dishwater and I knew then I could get on with my task, though I did wonder as I turned and rode on what my wife would make of such a costume.*

Tonight she told me she had not seen anyone, that no one called. I find this hard to believe, for I saw the young woman walk straight up our veranda steps and enter the front door without a pause.

Was I imagining the whole thing?

◇ ◇ ◇

Well, this is an appetite-whetter.

I have to force myself not to look ahead.

Already I am deciding that for the moment at least I shall not return these notebooks.

I go back to the first of them. The earliest entries covered a couple of years, mundane mostly, in their datings of arguments with bankers, fencing problems with neighboring farmers, descriptions—hardly lavish—of family celebrations, the noting of illness or windfalls. He confides his political ambitions to these pages and the dirtier workings of the Jericho Flats Council, the scams, the favors. (Nothing has changed, Gaden. Nothing.) The girls have left home by now, married to farmers in the Burdekin. His son has settled on a small holding close by.

But I am getting no closer to the man himself with grocery lists and quarrels with fellow shire council members. Does his baritone no longer delight at local soirées? Then suddenly I come upon an entry (it is now two A.M.) some weeks or so after my first encounter with him in the archives. When I say some weeks I refer, of course, to that point of congruency, ninety years away to the day.

January 8th, 1899. Another year. Decision made at last. We must sell this place. Apart from bad seasons, I feel something pulling me away from farming. It's a thankless business. Perhaps I am not suited for it after all. It was the sort of dream anyone might have who came from the sort of background that bred my parents in industrial England. It's telling on me now, both those stories of deprivation back home

and the social deprivation of the backblocks here. I have a hunger for a more active life among people. A better life. Politics is the place. It is not as if it will really affect Betsy. But it is as if forces beyond me are advising. How can a reasonable man write this way? Last night I lay awake half the night wondering how Betsy will react if we move to a town. Thank God it isn't a question of the children. They were so used to running wild. That's one thing about the country, the space. We'll have to see how this season goes and if things don't improve, I might even be forced back behind some bank counter. Percy told me I should have changed over to sheep in the last drought. When I finally went to sleep I dreamt Betsy walked into the council chambers wearing trousers and shocked everyone and even while I tried to lead her out she argued soundlessly with me, her lips moving but no words coming. I was reminded of that moment last year in the paddock.

I riffle pages.

That's a lie.

I gobble every word.

However . . .

February 28th. Spent a week at the coast assessing job prospects, crawling to the bank who hold a mortgage on this place and trying to persuade Tomlins' Stock Agency to come out next month and give me a fair valuation if I decide to put the farm on the market. Whatever I sell it for, our debts will wolf up profit. (Wolf up! I like that. A way with words.) *I did notice how many farmers on the coast have changed from*

cattle to cane. They all tell me there's better money to be made that way. But it's backbreaking work, too, and now they've stopped importing Kanakas, it's hard to get cutters cheap.

March 1st. I was very restless this morning on my last day in Rockhampton. What a hot little town it is, cradled among hills, gasping for a sea wind (Gaden, it could be me writing) *it never seems to get. Walking the town's streets this last week, I found myself dreading going back home even though R. is noisy and hot. I can't understand this. I am longing to see the family again. The girls are visiting.*

Glimpses, repeated, of a young woman whose face is familiar and unknown at the same time. That moment in the paddock? Her hair is almost white. I tried to catch up with her yesterday as she walked along the road by the river but to no avail. She turned into a side lane before I could reach her. What drew my eye, I suppose, were the clothes she was wearing—a flowered blouse like Betsy's best and a hat with the same sort of ribbons. Then an even stranger thing happened. As I sat in the River Rose restaurant having scones and a pot of tea, there she was again at the end of the room, facing me at a table near the street door, sipping a glass of water and staring past me. Through me, is what I mean, to the kitchen section at the back. I looked away for a moment to speak to the waitress who was bringing me some jam for my scones and when I looked back the table by the door was empty, cleared of all traces of customer. "Miss," I asked the waitress, "miss, was there a customer at the front?" The poor thing looked at me blankly. "Near the door," I insisted. "Just a minute ago." She shook her head. "You must be seeing things," she said.

I felt dizzy. Had I imagined this? Is it the heat? Am I

coming down with some illness? I couldn't help being sure because her dress, when I was up closer, was so like yet somehow different from Betsy's. The pattern on the blouse was much the same but the sleeves were short. She had them rolled well up and the skirt was high above the ankles. Outrageous really. (Do I write "outrageous" because one day Betsy might read this? She knows I have an eye for a pretty ankle. Perhaps that was why this stranger drew my eye in the first place.) Outside that steamy little café the sun was like a curse. I have never really grown acclimatised. The rank grass on the footpaths stank of horse dung. Too close a reminder of the farm. Something must be done.

Was it that day in the paddock?

Yes, I whisper in this stuffy hotel bedroom. Yes, it was then.

I read on. I am beyond sleep.

March. April. May.

June 12th. Yesterday the mailman brought a letter with good news. Sold up at last! In two or three weeks Betsy and the boys who have come over to help will leave for Mackay and I'll follow in a week after the new owner has settled in. Poor chap. He's a raw fellow who seemed to know very little about farming when he came out to inspect the place. I feel deeply for him and his family, but it's dog eat dog in this country I've discovered. Every man for himself. I have a fortnight before beginning my new job with the shire council. I suppose those years in the bank persuaded them and the work I did as a councillor for Jericho Flats. Will I be able to perform well? I think so. Oh I do think so. My nights are crammed

with dreams of a future that opens out into a great township. Brisbane, perhaps, and houses, so many houses it is almost a nightmare. And shopping mobs—that is the only word—rushing blindly about. Now and again in these dream crowds I catch sight of sunburnt arms and a swatch of fair hair and that strangely distanced young woman's face. I am certain now about where I saw her first. Certain. It was that morning as I rode out to shift the milkers. The morning I saw her walk straight into our house.

My dreams worry me. I am beginning to feel disloyal to Betsy. Oh for a new start. I am longing for it. It's not as if the girl exists. I badly need this change.

It is nearly three in the morning. Mr. Lockyer is farewelled at the Percys' farm with a supper party for all the neighbors. Persuaded to sing, he launches into "Take a Pair of Sparkling Eyes," with Mrs. Percy on keyboard. I see him, I see him, one hand resting lightly on the piano in the manner of the time, the other thrust into waistcoat. Men appear most vulnerable when singing, and I am hoping for an innocent abroad.

My eyes keep closing on this man's destiny that I am determined to make my own. I fall asleep in a pointillism of memories and wake up as a huge question.

How did Mr. Gaden Lockyer achieve his wife?

How does anyone achieve a wife?

It's ridiculous, when you think of it rationally, that women rush so gladly like Gadarene sows into a life of servitude. It's not that you need marriage for sex or breeding. Is it because men have cunningly put about the notion that spinsterhood is a bad joke, the old maid to be pitied? Who wants to be a butt? Who wants to be the fall guy?

Seb said to me a month or so after we had worn the candlelit dinner ploy to a frazzle, "My dear"—and I can recall each one of his devastating words with the chill I should have experienced on hearing them—"given the fact that I am thirty-seven and assuming I have forty years ahead of me, would you be prepared on a permanent basis to cook me fourteen thousand six hundred dinners, the same number of breakfasts, give or take a few? I'll see to my own lunch," the generous fellow added. "And do approximately two thousand loads of washing and ironing, housecleans and shopping?"

"You are suggesting marriage?" I asked demurely.

"I suppose I am," Seb said.

"It sounds enormously attractive," I heard myself say. "Is there a large salary to go with the job? Will I be full time? Shall I pursue my current career as well?"

Is my irony too richly stressed?

"I had rather hoped," Seb said with his delicious smile slipping a little to one side, "that you might keep on with your job. It really is a two-income economy, you know, and we'll need the money."

The cunning dog has turned it into a joke that barely conceals the real, the serious intent of his request.

"You make it sound irresistible," I said. "How could I refuse?"

"Don't be like that. I'm trying to be honest."

That was the horrible thing. He *was* being honest. He meant every arithmetical total.

Figures like that present a monstrous challenge. It was apparent I must break down those figures into smaller aggregates. Why not marry? I wondered. Marriage had become such a meaningless ceremony in the quickie divorce zone. Why not? It might be a pleasure to reshape his expectations and demands. Cynical, you might call me, but children of the eighties are confronted with a world that makes their lips curl.

My reshaping program was only partially successful. Seb sulked and ate out. I cried and burnt chops.

Once during an armistice I had asked him about his family. For a bride of three months I knew surprisingly little.

"How many kids in your family, Seb?"

"Four." He is reading *The New York Times Book Review* and hates being disturbed. "You know there were four. Three boys and a girl. Gloria was the eldest."

Poor kid, I think. Poor poor kid.

I probe more deeply and Seb slams down the paper. These were early days in the reshape program.

"Four nicely spaced. Two years between each of us. Mother died when Jumbo was eight."

Jumbo? Gloria? None of his relatives had come to the wedding, Seb explaining their absence with brief throwaway lines. When cornered he always became mono-word cryptic.

"Jumbo?"

"He was the youngest. Bit of a drag for Gloria when mother passed on. She had to leave school. Couldn't manage it and us. Shame, I suppose. She was rather bright. She did everything for us."

"Except have a youth?"

Seb smiles his brilliant smile. "Not sure what you mean, my dear."

"You know perfectly well what I mean. She must have spent just about every minute washing your school uniforms and cooking your meals. That's not much of a youth."

"We were a very close family," Seb says, smiling threateningly. "Very close. I don't know, Belle, whether you understand the concept of family. God knows with that scatterbrain mother it's a wonder you grew up normal. Well, almost normal.''

''Where's Gloria now?'' I ask.

Seb hesitates. I detect a variety of lies beginning to shiver into formation on his lips. Finally he admits, ''I don't actually know.''

''I thought you were a very close family.''

''Don't chop logic with me,'' Seb says nastily. ''I said we *were*. Gloria did something pretty unforgivable, really. Three years after mother died she left home and went nursing in Victoria.''

I laugh and laugh. I can't help it.

''She used to send a card at Christmas,'' Seb goes on ignoring me, ''but we never saw her again. And then two years after that we heard she'd married one of the interns.''

Hooray for Gloria! My silent cheers must have been audible to Seb's foxy ears for he pulls a face.

''And how did you cope with Gloria gone?''

''Father got in a housekeeper.''

''He could have done that in the first place, couldn't he?''

''Housekeepers cost, dear. They cost. We weren't made of money.''

''Poor Gloria.''

''Poor Gloria nothing. She's done very nicely, thank you, from all I hear.''

What does one say to spiritual blindness?

The brothers?

''Scattered,'' Seb says. ''Scattered. ''Is it really important that you know?''

''Not important. Just mildly curious. You're the one extolling the family unit.''

"U.K. The States. Jumbo got two years for burning his draft card. When I wouldn't bail him out he severed all relations. Satisfied? He's working on a daily in Southampton. Luke's a biologist in Houston. Got that all sorted? We write. Sometimes. Luke and I write."

"And your dad?"

"God, Belle, regular little ferret, aren't you? The dad's in a very expensive, very luxurious retirement home in Sydney. He plays bridge and bowls and he's doing fine. No, we don't see each other often. I go down about once a year. Now are you satisfied?"

About?

Satisfied is not the word I would have chosen. There was such aridity, such desolation in this rapid-fire résumé of Seb's family history, I was inclined to discover a new warmth and interest in my own. Pondering these imponderables I wept and wrote a long and foolish letter to mother who rang back and wasted a fortune as I howled long-distance. I hung up the receiver and tears, marveling about the nature of idiosyncrasy, whether the refusal to conform made life easier or more difficult. Whatever case I examined, I came up with only one answer: screwballs had it made. *Quod erat demonstrandum.*

Seb responded to my plea for sharing with a nasty and chilly sarcasm that demoted and reduced me: he took up what I can only call "men's cooking"—the infinite search for the perfect sauce—and whenever we had guests (oh, those *longueurs* of summer evenings on shaved lawns under the trees) insisted on preparing the entire meal, rejecting all offers of help, so that with the serving of each course he could discuss with Frank Hassler in boring detail the exact chopping, flavoring, cooking and timing methods.

"Belle's a chop and two veg woman," he would announce to gasping groups when he produced yet another triumph. "We've swapped roles. But she does a good mow job, I think you'd agree."

Was there something dog-in-the-mangerish about my resentment? I wilted under phrases like "the merest dash of fennel, not a smidgin more than an ounce of rum at this stage, pan broil for the quickest three minutes you've ever seen." At these parties the great Australian division of the sexes still took place but now the men spent their time trading hints for choux pastry while the women—well, the women, relegated to the backblocks of gastronomy, talked concerts and theater and on the home front, as the men would say, the best ways to clean out rain-gutters and grease-traps. Absorbed in their new authority and involved in inventiveness the men recommended dishes discovered on business trips or at conferences in out-of-the way places like Anchorage, Paramaribo, Sandakan.

I cannot see Gaden Lockyer interested in the properties of *empadade camarao* or even the four-egg sponge.

Would I have been different nine decades back? Would I have plunged into Betsy's role with the sacrificial joy those times expected, tendering daily offerings to the teeth father?

I still have a photograph I took one late afternoon of Seb and friends in a huddle over the traditional way to prepare *moussaka*. Their faces have a glittering intensity their wives never elicited. It's the only photograph I have kept of my marriage.

The camera shutter is diabolically fast.

Some quirk of conscience niggles me as I drive blearily away from the pub next morning, the box of photographs and diaries stowed in the trunk. I have every intention of returning it but at a time that suits me and I leave instead an explanatory and apologetic note on newspaper letterhead promising to post back everything as soon as my research colleagues have assessed and notated. I cannot bear the thought that all that material, even those photos and letters that are irrelevant to my purpose, should go back to join the clutter in the horse shed.

I have my poster in the trunk as well, my friends of the people poster, and now one hundred and twenty closely written pages of not so intimate jottings and a sense of expectancy. Driving on to Mr. Gaden Lockyer's next life-stop which must also be mine, I repress the jabs of rationality that keep warning me of spectacular idiocy as I accelerate towards the coast.

Hello Comet Bluff Dingo. Goodbye. Hello Duaringa.

I have chosen this place for entry. It will be no random attempt and obsession convinces me I can make it. I thank God I am not attempting to fight my way back into the script-time of the *Decameron*, the *Canterbury Tales* or the *Iliad*. On the one hand the expense would be mammoth and on the other I suspect there would be unsympathetic foreigners who would know I was a suitable case for treatment. Proust would have understood what I am doing, or trying to do, and have given a long-winded cheer. I am doing it with all the finesse of the most private-eye, retaining mother's sense of fun and supplying ambience as I bucket over back roads with the car tapedeck playing Blossom Dearie chirruping "I'm Shadowing You." I chirrup along with her as my car devours miles of road on the way to Duaringa.

Although I discover the right location, there are only remnants of the old buildings, glimpsed as I drive along half a mile of fenceline to where the current farmer has housed himself in triple-fronted brick. The farmer's wife to whom I reveal only my researcher identity and a falsely claimed relationship to the first settler, giving my name as Lockyer, subjects me to a good ten minutes' probing before she reluctantly walks me across to the broken-down stumps and partly caved-in walls of the old farm. It looks now like an abandoned packing shed.

"There," she says. "The old place was there. My father built the present house after he bought the property."

I unsling my camera. Besides being a convincing prop, it is a meanly professional looking Ricoh automatic with shutter speed of up to one thousandth of a second and a 35-70mm lens. The price tag would have assuaged doubts. I line up the stumps, the decaying walls. I click away and wonder how much film I must waste in this foreplay to establish authenticity.

She's a carefully spoken woman who, after the diligence of her questioning, now seems unsurprised by the assaults on family history of female strangers. She tells me her father had lived in the old house for about fifteen years before he rebuilt and had used some of the timber for the new place. "There's not much left, is there?"

It is unreasonable to resent those fifteen years of what I regard as intrusion. I move away from her into my own silence and look.

Desolation.

I climb up onto the creaking and doddering remnants of floor and stand on what was once a veranda, staring past her at the view his eyes must have taken each morning. If I block out the sight of the present farmhouse with its gleaming white trim and cherry red roof and subtract the monied results of crop-duster attention that has given the paddocks a fearsome verdancy, I can find desolation without the building as well.

Or is it in me?

She looks up at me anxiously. Her eyes are still curious behind spectacles, her thin worried face all wrong in this landscape stupor. I step over to the doorway and stand where Lockyer must have stood. With one hand on the paintless frame supporting me, I nudge off my joggers, still laced, and then my socks.

I catch twitches of alarm on the woman's face.

"I'm getting the feel," I explain in my flattest voice. "Please understand. It's rather hard writing a report, even for research departments, unless I get the feel."

Why does she stay? The word "report" smacks of public service coma that should be sufficiently calming.

"Be careful," she warns, suddenly anxious. "There might be snakes as well as splinters."

I want my naked feet to tread in those long-gone places where he trod. The woman watching me is dreading a crazed alien thrust on her hospitality with broken leg or shattered ankle.

"I'll only be a moment." I weave lies that startle me. I rattle on about instructions from my employers, the importance of Gaden Lockyer as Member for Walla, commemorative articles. It is, I think, eight decades more or less since Mr. Gaden Lockyer became the Honourable Member for, and now, as my sacristan feet pad across to the hole of a doorway, we are united by something as close as the feel of cool old wood.

She appears relieved somewhat by my gabble. It has been delivered with a sufficiency of authoritative detachment and when I add that I would like to spend a little time taking more photos of the surrounding countryside as well as interior shots, she says well of course and asks can I find my way back to the house where she'll be putting the kettle on. I tell her I will probably have to go back to my car for more equipment.

I track her departure through disturbed air, through the scarlet quiverings of acalypha that hedge the farmhouse garden.

Gone.

I close my eyes and listen in to Gaden and his wife and children in this box of a dwelling, examining the hollows, not of the four small rooms but of life's demands. Standing by the battered tin recess of their cooking place, I listen in. More memories can crescendo through this old tin flue than ever came from Stanley's exponential horn. I listen in. Each speaker has a voice my heart recognizes and his is lighter than the baritone depths I would wish on him. Betsy is not the nagger I mean-spiritedly hoped for and by lamplight the table, set simply for their evening meal, speaks plainly to me. I want to join them.

Through one paneless window I see an outbuilding where, by some trick of shadow, the rusted roof becomes a chiaroscuro representation of a man's face, brushed out in that blurred style of portraiture of past centuries. The features approximate those of a clerk outside the Jericho Flats bank. I shake my head and the effect vanishes. I blink and it returns.

I go back to my car, open up the trunk and slide out the poster, my movements unfortunately furtive. Repressing the impulse to look at the house but conscious of eyes, for soothers I make play with a large clipboard that I tuck obviously beneath my arm. Then I carry everything over to the shack with my back smarting under inquisitive stares.

I stand twenty yards off and assess the situation.

I am going to get right into the picture.

Right in.

At this point I am sheltered from the farmhouse by a line of orchard trees that must obscure my actions from the glaring windows of the farm. There are enough protuberances on the rotting timbers of the veranda for me to tie my poster into position across the gaping doorway. Once more I go up the steps, unfold the poster and, by standing on some loose bits of lumber, manage to reach up and get the first tie in position. One sharp dagger of ironbark gashes my thumb. Blood creates a smear down the pictured margins of their shack, the clump of stringybarks and Betsy's skirt. I smudge away what I can and tie the other side into position. More blood dabbles. Heart-bleed. The poster flaps in a small breeze until I stabilize it by the bottom ties each side of the doorway. Better. Much better. So that when I turn, step back down the stairs and walk away into the tussocks of burr a little distance before again swinging round to look at Mr. Gaden Lockyer's settler hut, there they are, *en famille,* waiting on their veranda, togged up for the cameraman, holding their posed half smiles and their bodies for a second of biography.

I raise my own camera to them, whisper "Hold it!" and snap them.

God! The very sight of them makes my astigmatic eyes spill over and this natural mist, plus the non-specifics distance affords as I back even farther to the fenceline, gives them a realism that is shattering.

Can I now be seen from the house?

This isn't exactly as I had planned.

I should be dressed for the occasion in long skirt, shirtwaister and lace-up boots. But there is a limit to the outrages of trespass. Although these garments are in a bag in the car trunk also, I am not yet crazed enough to go back and put them on. The farmer's wary wife, whose name I have already forgotten in the speedy way in which I dismiss irrelevancies these days, might easily ring for the police. Could be so ringing at this moment.

My eyes are riveted on that family group (with whom I am shortly to dine) which buckles in the breeze on the veranda of the abandoned farmhouse.

I concentrate on them, on their oneness, their existence *then,* willing myself back and backforcing my thoughts towards that center until everything outside me is diminished and my mind lasers at unseeable speed towards the flaming expected core.

Abandoning this decade, this century, I move forward from the fence, telling myself and that watching wavering group that I am about to join them.

I have all manner of *sesames.*

I have held the hand of a grandniece and drunk from her cup.

I have dined with a grandson.

I have anointed the soles of my feet on the timbers of his floor.

I am surrounded by the stage props of a landscape still unchanged.

I lengthen my stride to trot, to sprint, running faster than time until I am hurtling forward up the veranda steps and hurling myself bodily through my paper hosts, making sure it is Mrs. Lockyer I obliterate, and I am gaspingly through beyond their startled faces to the other side in an empty room whose walls and floors bear the injuries of absence.

Nothing.

Nothing but a wood sliver in my foot and an overwhelming emptiness with a throbbing in my ankle where wood has ripped flesh, a trickle of blood, and pain for every reason.

The hollowness mocks me. There is absolutely no one, not even the sensation of anyone, there. I doubt my own presence.

Lucidity arrives in a cold splash.

When I turn about to push out through my rent family, the farmer's wife is standing below the veranda, her eyes wide and unbelieving, as she takes in the enormous portraiture.

"My God," she breathes. "My God."

I think she's on to me.

"It's nothing," I say. "A shame about the poster. I tripped. Look, it's absolutely nothing."

She doesn't believe a word I am saying and I untie the corners and roll my family up.

Not a word.

VII

◇

I refuse to admit to failure.

Driving on to the coast I examine my progress so far.

Gaden Lockyer's youthful workplace, the Jericho Flats Joint Stock Bank, had been submerged by a small supermarket and carpark—no frills and only family sized. The town map of Jericho Flats assured me of that. I have failed to enter his settler hut—and when I say "enter," I mean merge with.

Are the people I encounter beginning to regard me askance from the moment I open my mouth? I am certain I look less of a negative that I did at eighteen. One of Seb's husbandly jokes was to say, "You're so fair, Belle, it's as if you're not all there." Gales of manly laughter to follow.

As I stab my foot on the accelerator I comfort myself that I am a genuine quester probing the unknowns of a district's past. There was nothing strange about Fawcett or Amundsen or Stanley except their obsessions and a delighted public (cheers! cheers!) regarded their obsessions as commendable. Expansion of territory. Profits and spoils of colonialism. Scientific interest. All the shabby reasons with which political leaders manage to cloak their greed in glory. Make it personal and it becomes a bad joke, a laugh. What is lesser about my own exploration?

And hello coast, at last, Sugarville, and intolerable heat boring down on the lazy river between fields of sweetgrass with the whole plastic enclosing blue turning the town into a sauna.

In my Fawcett-Stanley-Amundsen role I pitch camp at a motel, shower, eat lunch in a vegetarian café that is playing headbanger tapes and make for the local newspaper and its files ready to flash my purloined press card. I am dressed for the part in tailored skirt and shirt and carry a business-like briefcase so that I can seduce their reluctance. An hour there reveals notice of daughters' marriages and a photograph of Mr. Lockyer presenting an award at the Chamber of Commerce. In the Historical Society's rooms above the School of Arts, the lode is richer. I am bemused by a studio portrait of ten town worthies taken against drapes. There's a mass of suit and vest and watchchain and unstated sweat, the faces disposed into expressions of forward-looking gravity, a preponderance of which is directed by Mr. Gaden Lockyer, the Member for Walla, center front row, who is fixing the camera with an ancient mariner eye of political purpose. Gaden, how could you?

Where is that quirk of a smile that directs self-mockery at the whole pretentious business?

Are you worried?

The moment when you are about to be attacked in Parliament for political graft is close.

Is it the man to your right or left for whom you achieve preference?

I dig more deeply and discover the gentleman on your right is a mill-owner for whom you have finagled ten new miles of roadway and rail-track and who has gratefully advanced you the money to move into a town house whose spaciousness and style would have been beyond your purse.

In fact, within another half hour I unearth two photographs of house and prize-winning gardens where the sweep of lawn and shadow velvet under the massed poincianas seems edenic.

Better, the back of the photograph has a faded inked address.

It is nearly six o'clock when I drive round in the stored-up heat of the day to find the right street and the right number.

The house is still there. My God, it's still there, still with its splendid garden but no sign of Mr. Lockyer and his wife, with their aging smiles, standing by the veranda steps as they had in that early photograph, her sunshade dipping against a clump of frangipani. It's what they call a genuine old Queenslander, roof pulled down like a hat brim over the wide cool verandas, set back in an acre of palms and hibiscus, its trellised porches half hidden by bougainvillea and allamanda vines. It has been loved right into this decade and its paint-slick graciousness would make any real-estate agent slobber. Parked across the road from its gate, eyeing its ecstatic green shadows, its almost timeless splendor, I am filled with a kind of lust myself, not to possess but to be possessed by. The roof is new, I can see, but gable and rail decorations have been preserved and even the broad flight of steps leading up from the purpling lawn, although perhaps replaced over eight decades of Wets, retains its essential sense of welcome. It is as if nothing has disturbed this place between then and now.

At this penultimate stopping place I sit and smoke a quiet cigarette, wondering if my parked car excites attention, if I will be cautioned for loitering. Lockyer's journal is stacked beside me on the passenger seat and I pick up the last of the notebooks and thumb through until I come to one of the later entries. It is now 1912. Now. Then and now. There is a Euclidean immutability about any day in any year. Moments capture their own immortality and remain, I decide, static.

. . . if a day in 1912 is drawn to meet a day in . . .

August 15th, he writes in that determined cursive I now know as well as my own nervous scrawl and which, I confess, I can counterfeit with accuracy, *today is the day I have decided to retire from public life. It has been decided for me. It is only seven years since I received the mandate of the electorate but I feel there is little I can achieve in a country so pig-headedly individualistic and conservative. I can't sleep. Betsy snores these days so I get up, make myself tea and take it out onto the veranda. This is the end of it, then. I am writing this between sips. In the morning dark, the odd lights from other houses prick out across the township and I sit here smoking my pipe and watching the garden, all those trees and shrubs we have tended so lovingly, assuming their daytime shapes.*

The hills are a long way off. There is a flatness about this town that exactly echoes my spirit. As the garden solidifies with sunrise, a small wind saturated with smells of cane and fish comes from the river. The last day. I have drafted my letter of resignation. I have explained my part in this latest business venture with regard to the mill. I deny completely any implications of self-interest or fraudulent handling of monies in the Chillagoe affair. Everything I did was for the ultimate benefit of this State. My letter will be posted today.

There are clouds like pink fish swimming above dawnlight.

I'm alone but feel not alone. I'm aware that the Opposition has its spies. Could they stoop so low as to watch my house?

Same day, night. There was someone watching me beyond the picket fence and as it grew lighter I walked down the path between the palms to look over the gate. Oddly enough I wasn't afraid. And there was no one there. No one, though I sensed someone. I could have sworn there was a shape across the trackway watching me at the gate and I was reminded of that time, so long ago now, when I imagined a girl or woman walking before me in the streets of Rockhampton, taking tea in the old café and vanishing. All my years telescope and blur as I weep. Thank God no one can see me. What has it all been for, this public life, to end so shadowed by the implications of disgrace? It's so brief. It's so nothing.

It's me watching, Gaden. Me.

The sun has opened up every shadowy cave in the garden before its last western plunge. Then it dies. I am aware how obtrusive my presence is, trying to pluck up the nervous energy of my idiocy to get out of the car, go through that gate and knock on that door.

Tomorrow, I tell myself. Tomorrow.

I've no excuse for this. I know next morning I have no excuse, though by now I've discovered the name of the present owner of the house and have prepared an elaborate fabrication for the telephone call I shall shortly make.

Journalists can intrude anywhere. My camera is glutted with film. Its shutter longs to wink at everything it passes. I might have mentioned that I have a press card borrowed from a nervous cub reporter. Well, actually, that's a lie too.

I didn't borrow it. She left it lying around in the canteen. I do wish that phrase it takes a thief et cetera wouldn't keep surfacing. I refuse to think of Gaden Lockyer MP as corrupt despite the fact that this country, from its very beginnings, has been built and thrives on scam and corruption.

Is there so much difference between then and now, especially as my now will soon be then; or his then my now, whichever way the day takes me.

Seb was always rude about journalists, perhaps because his was the sort of job that attracted no media attention. Television appearances have the gutsy force of public baptism. Made it! Criminals become folk heroes, victims scum. My amiable eccentricities must be regarded as merely amiable. Even mother has had her share of media attention if only from publications like the *Banana Bowl Weekly* or the *Dingo Express*. Criminals and eccentrics—that's what the media love. Once in Brisbane when I was a schoolgirl I went shopping with Aunt Marie who had arranged to meet me at the foot of the escalator in a large department store. As I stood there waiting for her return from another department, fingering the scarves, examining the perfume racks, I was stunned to see my aunt appear at the top of the escalator, survey the milling crowds on the midday ground floor and burst into song. My aunt has a rotund and thrilling soprano. She sang as much of "One Fine Day" as she could fit in before the escalator brought her to the bottom. Shoppers were riveted. They began to applaud. I slunk away to the street entrance, wanting to die.

Sorry, Aunt Marie. Sorry about that. I understand now. I really understand.

The current owner of the house is called Solferino. Signor Solferino is at work in his real estate agency uptown. Signora Solferino is at home and expecting me, though when her door opens on my twitching (it's only excitement!) face, "Yes?" she asks too curiously as if I am not what she expected. The door opened behind her displays the gleam of costly possessions.

I remind her of my call. I flash the press card. I repeat my telephone lies.

My paper, I explain, has been co-opted to do a series on beautiful homes of the north for *Belle, Vogue, Interiors, Architecture Now*. I make up a couple more titles as I go along. Merely utter the word "house" and add a superlative. This is socially acceptable pornography. "The articles we are compiling will be syndicated throughout these magazines," I say. "And we need pictures."

I'm taking a risk. Signora Solferino has the sharp look a real estate agent's wife needs. If I had thought this thing through more thoroughly, had known all the facts, I would have written weeks before. A spot of letterhead opens lots of doors.

She notes my Ricoh, my clipboard, my briefcase. I don't look like a mugger, I'm too much of a negative. But I could be the vanguard. Still, she invites me in. (When I want to be carried over the threshold!)

I hesitate skillfully. "Are you sure?"

We are doing, I tell her, ten houses only and hers is the only one chosen in this town. The melting point!

I detect a tailfin flicker of vanity and pleasure cross her expensive facial and "Yes, of course. Come in. Please," she says. "Really," she says.

After that thudder of an opener, I am barely aware of her.

I am entering Mr. Gaden Lockyer's penultimate front door and attaining—was it *his* center?—his career point of peak and decline.

The proportions of the room into which she leads me are beautiful. A wide hallway cuts the house in two but the rooms branching off are large and airy, I can see, looking past the elegant Solferino shoulder at other open doorways. I unstrap my camera, adjust various levers and timers and take several snaps, angling my lens at green-filled windows, half-opened doors, a swoop of archway between living and dining rooms. "Beautiful," I keep murmuring, giving her the word like a Valium shot. "A splendid example of its period. Absolutely splendid." I toss in terms like "finial," "architrave," "soffit." I put down my camera and draw small sketches of wooden ornamentation. Cautiously I mention historical interest and confess that this, too, will be background to the article.

"I don't know a thing about the earlier owners," the signora says. She pats glossy hair as if ignorance is virtuous. "My husband saw it as a good investment, what with overseas buyers coming here and so on. It wasn't really rundown when we bought it. Paul has a wonderful eye for a good buy."

I bet he had, I think nastily. And the signora isn't a bad buy herself with those leggy good looks and Poppeia profile. And I bet, too, he wears a gold chain and a silk shirt open to the navel. "That's Paul," she says, becoming matey, pointing to an overlarge family portrait in decorator tints and my God he does wear a gold chain.

Their flashy latinate brilliance makes me paler than ever.

"We had that taken in the garden just after we bought. Of course we probably won't keep the place, you know. Not with this market. It would be madness, wouldn't it?" I agree it would be madness. "Especially when Ricky and Francesca have finished school. I mean who wants a place this big?"

"Yes, who?" I agree. I am adjusting flashlights, checking distances.

"Do you mind?" I ask, snapping off two of her posed against the baronial table, a sop to her vanity. Then moving through the archway back into the hall I make quick complimentary sounds to cover the fact that I am photographing far too much, and really odd things like the angle of floor meeting doorway, ceilings, perceived glimpses of the back garden through a rear door.

I'm wrong, baby, wrong! You can never take enough photos, especially if you promise copies. She points out even better angles. She leads me to the master bedroom (her term), the children's rooms, the sun porch, the kitchen, pantry, bathroom and laundry. I snap the lot. Gaden is nowhere to be felt, not with her stagey animation, her shiny assurance.

She demands publication dates. Her eyes are a bold shade of brown and challenge.

I suggest a couple of months. "We're calling it 'Pioneer Splendour.' Do you like that?" She likes that. "You'll be sent copies, of course." She smiles. "But there are three more houses to do. Two in Cairns and one in Townsville. I'll certainly let you know. You've been more than kind."

She believes me.

"We've had the kitchen and bathroom done up," she says, "as I'm sure you noticed. Service areas are so important to potential buyers."

"Lovely," I murmur. "Lovely. But it's a pity in a way."

Her eyes harden.

"What way?"

"Well, we had rather hoped to feature the colonial struggler mum coping despite." We both laugh lightly at the idiocy of this. "What was in the bathroom when you bought the place?"

"You won't believe this," she says. "A chip heater."

I certainly believe her. I send mental messages to mother.

"But that would have made the most marvelous illustration! Coupled, of course, with what you've done. Arduousness of pioneering and all that. Drover's wife stuff. Wife chopping the kindling. I suppose you've read *The Drover's Wife?*"

"No," she admits. "I can't say I have. Best seller?"

"Sort of," I say.

"And I certainly haven't chopped kindling!" More pals-together mirth. Her hands are heavy with rings. She seems repelled by the idea of chopping anything.

"Do you know," she says, "that old heater's still up in the shed. We kept the shed. Color, you know. Paul had thought he might do the heater up and sell it. Those old meat safes fetch a fortune. Heaters! Well!"

I wish she would leave me. I want her and her money-gabble eliminated, dissolved. Her presence has emptied the house of all ghosts which, I suspect, are wavering outside windows and doors, longing for her absence. I take more photos of the refurbished kitchen (pine veneer and calico-look Formica), the back veranda as we walk across, the back steps with a sudden glimpse of Gaden Lockyer, once the signora has headed up the lawn, standing in contemplative fashion leaning against a supporting post, tapping his pipe out on the railing. Will he emerge in the developed film or remain a negative like me?

We move swiftly through the luxuriant garden to what was once a chicken shed.

"It's in there," the signora says, tucking rich tresses

back, pointing for my nosy camera and then becoming involved with a closer inspection of her nail lacquer.

"What is?" I have been distracted by the saddened face of my disgraced lover.

"The chip heater. I told you."

I am dragging the door open before she can even look up from her high-gloss hands.

The heater is so ancient it might have warmed water for Pliny's up-country farm. It certainly warmed water for Gaden and Betsy. Despite rust and years it retains its shape. The flue has been detached and is propped against the wall awaiting my next move. One of my hands, quite of its own volition, reaches out and strokes the firebox door, touching the knob his hand once touched.

"I'll buy it," I say instantly.

"Good heavens!" The signora tears her attention from a chipped plum talon. Has my approach been too crude? Or not crude enough? "I don't know about that. I'll have to ask . . ."

I squat on the earthen floor of the chicken shed and open the firebox.

"Seventy," I say. Things are becoming vulgar.

"Well," she worries.

"Eighty. Cash. Now." It is a mistake to bid higher with people like this. They attribute an unjustified worth when the value for the bidder is purely personal.

"Done," she agrees with a girlish flutter and light tinkle. "Done."

We seal the bargain with a coffee in the laminated kitchen which Gaden leaves the moment we enter. Her husband, apprised at his office of the sale, arrives within the quarter hour to help load the heater into the car trunk which refuses to close and has to be lashed with rope into a semi-shut position. The signor's teeth and chain both gleam as he gives my car's hi-gloss an over-familiar slap. He is assessing my blondeness rather too intensely.

"Looking for color, are we?" he asks unfortunately and with fulsome house-side manner. "Now if you were looking for real estate I could really help." His hand comes to pause on my shoulder and his wife watches his hand.

"The only place," I say, "that would interest me would be yours." I nod toward the bungalow behind us whose only horror is that he lives there and his hand shifts away.

"Half a million," he says lightly.

The three of us laugh nicely.

Their gross speculative presence has exorcised the very spirit of the place and threatens as well to engulf the tender fabric of my mood. The fusion I require can only come, paradoxically enough, with solitude. Or so I hope. This whole globe is patchworked with pieces of past that refuse decay. Or glitter with it.

Should I break in at some timely moment when they have left the house to its murmuring self?

I drive off into heat and fantastic speculation. It was not in that sumptuous garden that Gaden Lockyer ended his days. The house was burdened with his rise to power, his exposure and the terrible weeks of accusation and disgrace until his resignation. The years of retirement withered. Mr. Lockyer eased them out in a nursing home on the coast, enduring, so I believe, what St. Augustine deemed man's fall from grace—flatulence. As well, I don't doubt, there were problems with teeth, continence, the shakes, misty vision and faltering thinking. A classic case, as any medical man might say. A classic case.

It is another sixty miles to the last stop, last resting-place, landfall of Gaden Lockyer, bank clerk, farmer, local councillor, state Member, father of four, husband.

Descendants?

His line has died out more or less. I have met grandson and great-grandniece. Circumferences are disappointing. Anyway, familiarity breeds distance, have you noticed? A too-close involvement with a watered-down bloodline obsessed by mammon middens of the eighties would teach me nothing. I have a sizzling vision of archeologists hundreds of years from now unearthing a cache of Walkmans, digital watches, designer sunglasses, Italian jogging shoes, espresso machines and vertical grills. *Who?* his great-great-grandkids would ask. *Who? Him? Yeah, well. Maybe. Don't know all that much about him. Yeah. I believe he was my grandfather, great-grandfather, great-uncle, whatever. Bit of a scandal, wasn't there? Misappropriation of funds? Hell, they all do it! Old bastard, eh? Crummy photo, isn't it? God, all those hairies looked the same. Pity they didn't have Polaroids in those days, eh, then they could have seen how godawful they looked within minutes. Anyway, that would have been on mother's grandmother's great-aunt's side. Hell, it's a hassle getting across town to the job. Don't see so much of the olds. Sorry.*

No. I didn't want that. I was not anxious for question and answer (Socrates, you didn't know the half of it, either) to a background of monster post-teen stereo full blast by the barbie pit. No no no.

VIII

◇

I reach the little beach town of Tin River by two that afternoon.

It's a townlet of terminal attractiveness. White sand. Blue water. One street of small shops and an esplanade strip of park, coconut palms backed by a tatty line of holiday shacks, the artificial grass of a bowling club, an ice-cream parlor now closed, groves of mature she-okes and small headlands north and south like brackets.

Tin River is a parenthetic statement.

There are, as well, two blocks of holiday rental flats with beach towels dangling over railings and a six-unit motel with doors painted an ominous red.

I check in. Unhesitatingly I sign the register as Lockyer. I am convinced of my identity. My room smells of sadness and the sea and the hollow moments of people in transit who pulled in, stayed one night and moved on. I can only write what I feel or I think I feel. This place is so out of the way—a true funkhole for notoriety—the motel is still placing that "sanitized for your protection" strip across the lavatory seat, a strip I snap apart with a hoon's carelessness and crumple into the trashbin. There is a double bed with a faded tropic spread, an open wardrobe space with four bent wire-hangers, a television set bolted to the wall and curtains that match the bedspread and are even more faded. (I examine my face in the wall mirror and discover I have vanished.) My motel guide booklet has given the place two stars. Can't they count? I root around in the bathroom cupboards and find an electric jug and what the natives call "tea-making facilities." I tea-make, taking my brew onto the small terrace outside my room and sip away listening to sea-talk. Later I stroll along the main street in the screamer heat of afternoon, downtown one way, then back the other, half a mile each way. In a country with only a nomadic makeshift history there are few monuments beyond Returned Services League clubs and football fields, and here there aren't even these. There's a fish shop–café, a mixed grocery store and a newsagency.

In the newsagency, which also sells hardware, toys, beach gear and patent medicines, the management leans his fifty years against the counter as if he knows everything about this town.

"No," he tells me when I ask about the retirement home that used to be along the front. "Not anymore. Hasn't been run as one for years. Too awkward for the relatives to get down here with that gravel road in. Ruined their cars."

I ask when it closed.

"Late thirties I reckon. I don't remember too much. I was only a nipper. But the granddad moved into it round about then. The war changed everything. They shut it down when war broke out. As a retirement home that is. Couldn't spare the nurses, see. Most of the old folk were shipped back to Rockhampton. That's how it was."

"Is the building still standing?" I ask.

He looks curiously at me.

"You would have driven in past it. Big rambling place, two storeys, right down the northern end in a sort of cul-de-sac just as you swing in. It's easy to miss. It's a boardinghouse now. Not doing too good, I hear. The old girl who runs it depends on family trade in the school holidays. But there's a couple of regulars. Two old chaps. In a way it's much like it was, except the regulars don't get nursing care. Where you staying?"

I tell him.

"Yeah." I watch him computing this. "Well, that's a bit more up-to-date, I reckon."

"Everything is sanitized for my protection," I say and he looks sharply at me and asks, "What? What's that?"

"It's very comfortable," I lie. This is a small town. I must be verbally discreet. I might stay here longer than I planned. I might stay here. I might stay. "Very comfortable."

To placate him I buy a stack of postcards and a paperback I'm doomed never to read.

I cross the road and go down to the beach. Now I am here I can take my time. And his. It's a gently shelving strip of extraordinarily white sand at which the reef waters merely nibble as they did at Poindimié. Fifty yards out a lone fisherman is rocking quietly in a dinghy. So I sit on the sand, Gaden beside me, and look across the Pacific to South America. I have never been there but its dream quality is no less affecting than that of the elderly presence fidgeting on the dune slope beside me.

"How's Betsy?" I ask. "And the kids?"

But he doesn't answer.

"We're glum today," I say, shifting naturally into the nursing home jargon plural. "Don't we like it here?"

Turning diary pages. They are with me all the time now in a tote bag.

Look, it was true for Euclid and it's still true for me and

every geometry freak who lived since then. I am struggling to lay out a proposition that the past remains within the present, not even out of focus, the fragments simply repositioned by the disturbance of new presents and new pasts, everything jumbled and shuffled but extant: knowledge established remains, even if untapped.

I turn the pages of Gaden Lockyer's third little journal.

The year is 1922.

October 9th, he had written, the writing more spidery and tentative than I cared to see. Written at Tin River. *Unbearably hot today. Everyone says it is cyclone weather but it's too early in the season for that. Matron said I could take a walk along the front provided I wore my hat. My God! Telling me! Like a child. There was a time. . . . But it's quiet here in the four o'clock sun. I'm sitting under a patch of banksia scrub at the southern end of the little bay. Just to be free of those dinner smells and the smells of the other old and dying and the clackety clack of the nurses' tongues, chivvying like sheep-dogs, jollying us along. How I miss Betsy and Betsy's cooking. I think she died of my broken pride. Betsy could make a bare bone tasty.* (Well, good for you, Betsy!) *This home smells eternally of boiled beef.*

If I'm late back I'll miss tea. Not that it matters any more. They serve tea early so they can get us into bed and off their hands. God knows what the young nurses do when they've got us settled for the night. Go back to their cane farms and flirt with the cutters? There are only four of them and the matron. I long for some intelligent conversation but the only chance I have is when the doctor makes his monthly round from Mackay. He drives all the way down in his brand new Ford and I'm afraid he's not too bright either. Not as bright as his car.

Have I come to this, beached on nowhere, the stink of sugar and burning behind me simmering round the hills. The children never visit now. It's too far for them, too far from Brisbane. When our boy was wounded in the Dardanelles everything seemed to go wrong. He was never the same. And neither were we. They write. Oh the girls write, dutifully enough. But it was Betsy they cared for. It was Betsy they really worried about.

Perhaps I should have been seeking Betsy. After all, it is a center I crave. Does it have to be male? I think of mother and swim drunkenly in self-pity.

I leaf on, turning pages. There are a few entries for the next year, his last.

March 20th. I read the date and narrow my eyes into the sun skating across the waters of the reef. It is today's date. My body holds itself tense. *I'm on the beach again. There have been electric storms every day for a week now and flurries of rain that have done nothing to ease the heat and oppressiveness. This is my only escape, putting down what I know or think I know.* (That phrase jerks me upright. My hands tremble.) *If matron sees me writing, she'll want to know what I'm up to. Secret thoughts are like a disease to her. I do have the feeling someone has been looking through this notebook when I'm asleep. The pages feel touched. Matron treats me with that puritan righteousness the victim of a public scandal merits.*

She's back, that young woman, the girl I wrote about all those years ago. Today. This afternoon. As I sit here in my madness in the banksia shade, my eyes squinting against sea glare, she comes towards me from the other end of the beach even as I write, dragging her bare feet through water, digging a channel with her toes. Matron's husband is out there throwing a line for some retirement home dinner, on the first sunny day for a fortnight. Good luck to him. I wonder if he can see her. She's outrageously dressed, the way she was on that very first occasion, like a boy. I'm learning not only to live with this folly but to look forward—the paddocks, the tea-room in Rockhampton, watching from behind the fence in a Mackay dawn. (But it was evening, Gaden, evening for me!) *It's the same young woman. I'm used to that odd garb now. I'm ceasing to find it outrageous at all. It suits that boyish walk and look.*

Here she comes, swinging a straw hat by its strings and strolling up from the water, right up to where I'm sitting and I say good afternoon and she doesn't even turn her head. Her eyes go right through me as if I'm not here in a way that makes me blink and when I focus again she's gone. The encounter shocks me. I can feel my heart thumping too fast under this tough old hide. I'm imagining things, I know, yet why is it when I walk down to the water myself I find the tide already filling in her footprints?

Gaden, my dear, you're haunted.

What about me?

Beaches, I think, scuffing sand between my toes and trying not to remember Poindimié. Beaches.

Bonnie and Marie used to be taken to the coast once a year when they were small because grandma insisted they have a fortnight away from the inland heat. Grandpa left the head stockman in charge and they always rented the same house at Kirra, high on the dunes with only a fifty-yard sprint to the water. Those were the years just after war broke out. Every afternoon the family sunbaked while speakers fixed to the shark-watch tower spewed out popular music. *Oh Johnnie oh Johnnie,* lisped Bonnie Baker, decibel ten, *how you can love,* while oiled kids worked themselves into a frenzy for the sandgarden competitions, making designs with shell and pebble and weed. Or young women paraded each week on a rigged platform to see who would be Miss Kirrabelle.

No one played "The Rustle of Spring" over the speakers. Big bands challenged the firmament. Grandpa enlisted.

Grandma took the girls away each year on her own for the next three years. They sat on the sand and watched the beach-girl entrants.

"I want to enter," Marie said.

"I want to enter too," Bonnie said.

"Don't talk nonsense, you babies," grandma said. "You're far too young. But you're good looking enough," she added consolingly and a passing man winked at them on his way to the roped-off platform where he would wink at the beach-girls.

Grandma had laughed, twirling her sunshade.

"Men," she said. "Silly young fool. But if it gives him pleasure."

Years later I would say to Bonnie, "I want to enter."

The beach-girl competitions had moved from the sand to the clubs. Bonnie and Marie would be playing saccharine numbers to a mob of poker-machine-playing deaf mutes.

And Bonnie would say, "Darling, they're starting to look like tarts. No."

In the leeringly lit interiors of Leagues and Returned Services club halls the entrants were judged by elderly men with even bigger breasts than the competitors and certainly larger guts. I was appalled and fascinated by the obscenity of contrast.

I'm not your average beach-girl, am I, Gaden, sprawled out in the cruelty of reef-reflected sunlight and the coarse shade of dune scrub? But you keep seeing me as what?

Some nagging intruder pilgrim from another time determined to haul you into the corruption of the eighties? Could we show you a thing or two on graft! Would you be worse or different?

I am asleep before I realize, a candidate for sunstroke, and wake an irritable hour later with my legs badly burned, a rocking headache, outward symptoms that return me to my honeymoon. Shadows lie low on the cooling sand. Creakily I haul myself up, shake the grains from my clothing and limp back along the beach to the northern end, coming out to the roadway where the old boardinghouse squats in its rambler garden also staring at South America through weeping casuarinas.

A plump motherly woman is hosing fern clumps beside the front steps and beyond her I can see a kind of shadowy hallway and the rail of a second flight of stairs leading to the upper rooms. When I hesitate by the gate she looks up, nods pleasantly and makes some comment on the heat but I am too sun-drained to pursue inquiries and nod and smile back as I limp past and down the road to my beach-wrack motel which serves me dinner in my room. I can't eat. Television fails to distract. I am at the center—is it?—of my obsessional search, and there is no center. Or if there is, it shifts position, moves away as I clutch, eludes.

I still remember the definition of locus: *the curve or surface generated by a point or line moving according to specified conditions*. More simply, the locus of a point is the path traced out by it when it moves in accordance with some given law.

Problem: plot the locus of the point that represents Mr. Gaden Lockyer, MP. The locus must be restricted to those central issues that made up his life and must not concern itself with marginalia.

I ignore the steak chips lettuce and thawed-out slice of cream cheese pie and on my clipboard write out the following problem as I see it: Find the locus of the intersection of straight lines which pass through two fixed points on a circle (Gaden, we do share a circumference of sorts!) and intercept on its circumference an arc of constant length.

I fiddle round with this for twenty minutes. I reword my problem another way: G and B are two fixed points on the circumference of a circle and PQ is any diameter. Find the locus of the intersection of PG and QB. (And having found it, will my car, will I, manage the distance to be traveled?)

The mechanics of *quod erat demonstrandum* are simple enough.

It's the quality of my assumption that worries me.

I place my uneaten dinner back on the tray and put the tray outside my door. Not even one star for the dinner.

The journal in one hand. Geometric hieroglyphs in the other.

Oh god oh god oh god.

Since leaving Seb I have become a talented insomniac. Relief in life-styles has made no difference. At one, three, five A.M. I am to be found any night making coffee and staring into space. I am to be found now in the three A.M. depression zone, body flow at its lowest like the sea seen through my nighttime door, the curtains on my window drawn back to let in the phosphorescent light of water whose breaking lines look like radiant tubes in the dark. Desolation. I need party time, cheer, goodoh, how y' goin, where y'been—all that whacko stuff.

And where have I been?

I refuse the answers.

Seb was a rotten party man. He liked the small intellectual half-dozen he could dominate.

I keep remembering.

Six years ago, Bonnie, in the first flush of alternative rustic living, decided to throw a birthday party for Stanley. His aged relations and cronies from coastal towns as far away as Cooktown were contacted but only one group replied. Bonnie filled in gaps with fellow-feelers from the valley. The relatives from Brisbane were expected at lunchtime for this day-long fest. Mother had gone to a lot of trouble. She had been working for a week. The place groaned with vegetarian dishes. To cope with the overflow of guests, as it were, she had a cesspit dug well back of the house ("Belle, dear I almost prefer it to the press-button!") surmounted by a stout timber lavatory seat, the whole convenience concealed by hessian walls tacked onto bush poles. A tin of lime and a bowl of water for hand-rinsing were placed with designer flair on a stump next to the lavatory. "Who needs the furry toilet cover with musical toilet roll?" Bonnie demanded of the sky. "Let's give those townies a taste of the real thing!" There was even a fire-pit for cooking the meat she felt she had to offer carnivores and bush tables knocked together by Stanley.

The stack of liquor amazed even Seb.

"Bring the kids," Bonnie had invited expansively. "Everyone's welcome."

By midday things were going with a zing, all the guests so far being farming or pot-smoking neighbors and their gate-crashers. At one, after all the dishes had been mangled and most of the meat devoured by lip-servicing vegetarians, a sleek BMW rolled up the track and a pair of denim clad swingers with two nose-pickers in tow climbed out and introduced themselves as Stanley's nephew and wife from Brisbane.

Bonnie exclaimed with pleasure greetings even as her eyes made reservations but she rushed about filling glasses and plates and making sure Stanley took the newcomers under his care. By this time food supplies were running low so she went back to the shack and returned with a couple of dishes she had been keeping in reserve for latecomers. Mr. and Mrs. Denim accepted graciously, their children whined and demanded ice cream ("I'm sorry, darlings, no ice cream!") and started whacking at plants with sticks.

"Please don't do that," Bonnie asked nicely.

"Why?" the boy demanded swinging blindly with his stick. It caught Bonnie on the shin.

"Naughty, darling," Mrs. Denim reproved.

Mr. Denim asked, "Could I have some more wine? And another glass. This one's dirty."

"Help yourself," Bonnie snapped. "Your child has just broken my leg."

"Well!" Mrs. Denim said. "Well! I mean really!"

Later, on the point of departure, Mr. Denim took Bonnie to one side. "Look," he said, "if you're going to do this sort of thing professionally, you'll have to do a lot better than this. Catering is a specialized industry. And the lavatory is atrocious! Atrocious! My God, you can't take kids in to that!"

At that point Seb had moved in on him with his beatific smile and supreme vowels and hissed softly, "Listen, you mean-faced bastard, Bonnie is not a servant. She's your hostess. She's worked all week to get this thing going for your uncle, all bloody week. As a friend. Why don't you try to set your loathsome kids an example, say thanks and then piss off."

I think that was the only time I genuinely loved Seb. These days I unwillingly recall that party and admit Seb has his points.

Later that evening, the party evening, her legs stretched out to the fire, one shin dabbed brown with iodine, Bonnie became forgiving. "Townies, dear," she kept saying. "Townies. Never been off the bitumen."

Then the real party got under way. Those wonderful fag-end stayers. We delighted each other over the vision of the defeated Denims leaving the scene in bursts of dust and carbon monoxide, and a doped-out young male from the valley told us how he had streaked across Europe. "Lecce to Alborg," he said modestly. Georgio was a muscular marijuana grower and professional protester whom Bonnie had met when they were both lying down in front of bulldozers. He had been arrested, he told us, in Naples, Assisi, Rome, Milan and Lausanne where he cheated a little and took to the leafier sides of the highway.

"Why were you doing this?" Seb wanted to know.

"No reason, man," Georgio said. "Just for kicks."

By Frankfurt his fines totaled thousands but by then, too, a sympathy faction had formed and was paying them. He also cheated by not being entirely naked but wearing Reeboks. The Black Forest was a disappointment because of dieback and he was arrested six more times before reaching Hamburg. By then he'd made the newspapers and achieved such amused fan support there were cheer-on headlines: Streaker reaches Vejle! He was getting bored with his own fame. The danger had slipped away and he was condemned to run naked right up into Denmark with the weather beginning to bite. But he was modest about his notoriety, denying he wanted help, preferring those days when his flight from motorcycle police who were only halfhearted about it anyway, forced him to swim canals, streams, rivers. Near Alborg he came down with a severe cold but ran sneezing and naked into the central square to the woolen-clad hurrahs of youth. "It was a first for Australia," he said, hogging more of Bonnie's claret. "A little something for the bicentennial. I had a flag painted on my bum."

I think of this. I think of my own crazy flight backwards. I think of Seb, his mouth curved in delight, listening to Georgio, and I am still awake by four.

The moon has floated beyond the zenith and is like a huge communion bread, chaste in the navy blue air. During the afternoon someone must have checked in to the room next to mine for through the thin walls I hear coughing and the noise of their toilet. At this moment even the heavy breathing of a body in a bed right next to the wall is audible. I try not to clatter as I make myself more coffee and sit, a bedraggled Euclid neophyte, examining a muddle of journey-lines no more emphatic and as content-less as the streaker's, a journey that has achieved nothing. I admit it. Q.E.D. Perhaps sanity is returning after an obsession that has endured a foundered marriage (or that I used as an excuse to scuttle it), a change of jobs and what appears to be a fruitless search for the other half.

Other half?

Center?

Whatever.

Huck, father, shriveled with fright perhaps, after my discovery of him, had written once. He wrote also to mother but both communications displayed no more affection than that of a penfriend.

The other half? The imagined other half? Horace, you too, I say classically joking, you didn't know the half of it, and the joke, limp as it is, blows through my mind like some cleansing salt stiffened wind and I roll over on the tangled hot sheets and inexplicably fall asleep.

It is nearly six when I snap awake and sit waiting for the sun's red stain to spread all along the eastern rim. Palms, shrubs, dune-banksia are rags against dawnlight. If I were dumped suddenly, I wonder, eyes peeled of bandage, how would I know immediately whether it were night or day without waiting to see light wax or wane?

As I wane.

An hour passes and breakfast is delivered and after, when I open my motel door on the beach side, the gulls clatter in from the water screeching and propping, eyeing the scraps on the plate in my hand.

Behind the gulls, the bay lies flat as another plate.

I pick up the uneaten bacon, shred it and flip the pieces into an excited weaving of wings and stabbing beaks. The squawking of the birds rips the morning air like paper and a small girl comes out of the unit next door in her pajamas and stands staring. There must be sixty gulls by now, a terror flock. The food gone, the birds fall silent, watching, jerking closer to the tiny patio with its plastic mold furniture, one of them flapping cheekily onto the table.

I am reminded of me.

I pick up the last pieces of toast and toss untidy lumps skywards. The shrieking begins again and the small girl shoves a finger in each ear in an exaggerated way and makes a yuk face. Her freckled nose is critical. "Mummy can't sleep," she says.

"No one can," I reply, my eyes on one bird at the front of the flock, so like me, so like me, that jumps, automatically paralleling each upward swing of my arm and the hopping of the other birds, and always misses. Out.

It always misses. It can never get into the picture. Not

like those crows of the mind whose offstage raspings dominate and shred landscapes empty of everything except the family outside the settler shack, the clerks outside the bank, the one-storey towns huddled beside slow coastal rivers.

"Here," I say, kind, aiming toast directly at this gull. "Here." And I feel that personal wrench each time it jumps and fails to catch the bread as another gull swoops in.

There is nothing more to do, nothing more I can do. The bayside township sits along its only road, still half asleep, damped down by rain during the night. The trees along the front drip from their needlelike leaves, blurring the picture, blurring the mind. Broader leaves make handprints across the sky. My eyes are the camera shutter now but the film doesn't roll. I snap the same scene over and over.

There is no center to this circle. And if I construct or try to construct radii from where I stand I will find there is no circumference or, if there is, its margins are so mistily distant they can never be reached.

Back inside I pack my night gown, camera and spare underwear and slinging the canvas carryall over my shoulder walk into the morning, ignoring my car as it noses affectionately up to the motel doorway and, resisting the temptation to fling my car keys into the sea, walk south past the shops until I come to a small seafront reserve where there are two benches and a table facing the water. I sit there, the sun well up now, and already I am perspiring in the eight o'clock weather stew, sensing damp from the wooden slats seeping into my clothes. But it is more than perspiration that damps my forehead, a kind of fever at crack point. I can only describe what I suffer or imagine I suffer.

Across pewter water a fishing boat crawls in to the co-op store by the pier. This might be my last throw, I decide, the last place I can bear to tread the stubborn rituals of search. Or bear to be. That is what frightens me. "You're crazy," Seb had remarked softly and in such a kindly and dispassionate way on the morning I left him, I am inclined to believe him. "You're a monomaniac bitch."

The slammed front door failed to obliterate his last words.

"Arms," she had begged the empty air of River Terrace. "If only arms, yours, Seb, or someone's, genuinely clasping. Safety."

Can I put the blame for my failure to prove the riders of self-evident truths on the clichés of convention—those stereotypes presented as the prose of living? Once they maddened me. For years I had attempted to counter them, especially with Seb and especially with his superior macho pals. Everything about my dim existence strengthened my resolve to eschew feminine strategy. Tough as his buddies. Swapping vile joke for vile joke. Searching for the aggressive male simile with the same energy as an ad man, especially in what we call the months of spring as the girls in their summer dresses devastated Seb's roving and particular eye with the same boring repetitiveness of male poets discovering breasts thighs vulvae in the most banal of landscapes. Gritting the teeth of my mind.

"I don't like this," Seb had said. "I don't like it at all. What are you trying to prove? You're making yourself conspicuous," he adds in his old-fashioned way.

"I thought you liked a bit of intellectual dash."

"Is this intellectual? This shadow boxing?"

I become louder, to irritate. Inwardly I am hugging my solitariness for comfort, like sucking a thumb. Once Seb tried to run away from me as we argued our way through Brisbane town, springing onto a bus that took him away from home rather than toward. Later, he pleaded with me, acknowledging defeat. "Give it a rest, will you? You're way ahead on points."

Behind the thinnest of smiles I had replied, "Your lot never give it a rest. Can't you take it? I'm only just starting. Only starting."

Now it's ending. This is it, the vernal aphrodite commencement of day. And realization.

I wriggle stiff limbs on the hard seat and stand up, stamping my feet to get the blood moving. The sea's blood, too, is on the turn and beginning to ripple in bar-lines across the sand, the same old tune. Mournfully I find myself humming, *tempo maestoso,* "The Rustle of Spring," which, Bonnie once admitted, was the piece she played for Huck just before he proposed. I think of this and turn my musical offering to the day into a *marche funèbre,* for that is what it is.

As I walk back down the main street, the township is yawning and stretching. Dogs and children and old men are out. The early risers. The newsagent is hosing down the footpath and I go in and buy the paper of the day before, which is the latest news of the outside world to reach Tin River, and nod to his recognition and walk out and on, uncomfortable in my damp clothes, along past the fish café, the closed ice cream parlor, past the bowling green, the motel with my car still snoozing outside unit five, the boutique some wit has called Get Frocked, the mixed grocery with real estate notices in the window, the weatherboard church of uniting denomination.

The town ends imperceptibly like so many towns in this part of the world, and becomes a scatter of beach shacks tailing along the road to the northern arm where the old boardinghouse waits for me.

I am back at Villa Marina. I am back.

The plump landlady whom I spotted yesterday is packing odds and ends into her car trunk. There is that unmistakable landlady look. What is it? Mrs. Moody had it. It's the confidence of ownership combined with the anxiety of one always fearful of a tenant's moonlight flit. As I draw closer I can hear her calling advice and orders to someone inside and whoever it is emerges, another middle-aged woman geared for a day's shopping in town nearly sixty miles away.

Even as I draw level with the driveway gate, they have creaked jokily into the car, buckled their seat belts and begun to reverse and turn. The driver is watching me in her rear vision mirror but I conceal my oddness and my anxiety and my knowledge of failure under a bright fixed smile to which she suddenly responds and I keep walking past the building towards a narrow bush track into the seafront scrub until the station wagon fades along the curve of the road.

I walk back.

The big sprawler of a place seems empty.

I wait—one minute, two—then go through the gate and up the path between casuarinas, up the steps onto the veranda and knock on the still open door. This knock is phony. It's soft. I don't want anyone to answer. I want, last fling of the dice, to go through into that shadowy vestibule and hallway which will have the reassuring familiarity of all rented houses, the dusty half-life of all the rooms I have ever lived in, with only my few mobile possessions to establish identity.

Silence falls from the air.

I go in.

A staircase with polished worn treads leads to a half landing, performs a dogleg turn and mounts to the upstairs corridor. The landing is lit by a window of clear glass panes through which I can see the unmoving leaves and florets of a flame tree. In the hall there is a bench more appropriate to a church, a darkly varnished occasional table with a bowl of hibiscus and two rattan chairs.

I sit.

I am not sitting to plan my next move.

There is no next move.

As far as I can ascertain or with chewed pencil stub worry at the ramifications of theorems 27 and 28, Euclid Book I, I have reached a point of no return and from now on can only absorb.

The whole place feels rinsed out but I am wrong for there's the sound of someone tramping in from the backyard. Rooms away a door shuts with a thud and feet plod down the corridor right-angled to where I am sitting, my back to the wall.

He's a yardman of sorts. Or a wilting guest. He's in rubber boots and old gray twill trousers muddied at the knees and he smells of grease trap. He looks gently withered and fifty or sixty or even two hundred. Perhaps he is the husband of the landlady. His face is not suspicious, simply tired.

"Hello," he says. "What can I do for you?"

This is a metaphysical question. I know there is nothing anyone can do for me. I must deliver a mollifying lie. Or half lie.

"I'm waiting for someone," I say.

You see, I have not lied.

"She's just left," he says. "You missed her. Gone up to town for the day. She won't be back until late."

"That's all right," I say.

In this dusky vestibule my shocking fairness must make me the very essence of a negative. He is peering as if trying to adjust focus.

"Were you wanting a room?"

I had thought of this. It is probable I will want a room, a berth in Gaden Lockyer's last port. Oddly, at this moment, I find I am weary of the search. Its poignancy vanished during the night and that absence was reinforced by the sight of my alter-ego gull swooping for food and missing. I am conscious of emptiness and exhaustion as if the ardor with which I became a hunter has burnt down to a little fine ash.

Irrelevantly I recall—was it two years ago? three?—Frank Hassler expansive at party time putting forward his theory that man came closest to solving the problem of perpetual motion by using women. He had waved one explanatory hand with a stuffed olive in it while he told the rapt group how his eighty-year-old dad had gone into shock after his wife died. No, not grief, Frank explained. He simply didn't know how the stove worked. Imagine—and we all imagined—he'd been an industrial chemist for fifty years and the mystique behind the browned chop and the creamed potato eluded him. The women's laughter, I remember, was tinged with sourness. I sit here understanding my own whirling motion—the kind of detail-craving mania that makes women the natural choice for any nit-picking job (Hassler: *Forgive us, my dear. The male brain is too large to cope!)*—was running on worn cogs.

The yardman waits patiently for answers.

"Possibly," I admit. I am very tired. "As I said, I'm waiting."

He regards me with an odd sideways turn of the eye. He grins.

"So are most of us."

I look past him down the corridor Gaden Lockyer knew.

The old man persists. "Anyone in particular? You've got to be waiting for someone."

I cannot possibly say, can I? Or can I? I will offer a name and it will mean nothing. Lockyer, I tell him. He gives his head a shake and farther down the passageway at his back a door creaks open and I see an elderly woman flitter towards what might be the kitchen. I am reminded of Mrs. Burgoyne.

"No one of that name. Not living here."

"I wouldn't actually call it living," I reply with surprising energy and he looks at me as if I have been offensive. Surely exhaustion has rendered me harmless enough.

"Everyone's out bar old Mrs. Luck and me. The wife's up the coast like I said. No one's due back till later."

I drop my eyes. He's not the yardman. I would have taken a bet that he was a nosy resident whose empire had extended beyond his rented room to a garden kingdom, but I'm dealing with authority here.

"Don't mind me," I say. "If it's all right, I'll just wait here. I'll be all right."

"You can't do that."

"Why not? Mr. Lockyer has—has booked in. They'll know about it, you'll see. Your wife will know."

Our eyes lock in challenge. I see his waver.

"Suit yourself," he says. "You've got a long wait."

He shambles off. Exit, retainer, right. Correction, husband.

The wall to the right of me suddenly gasps with sunlight as he opens the door to the back garden. Somewhere a radio crackles with static and the nine o'clock news. He'll be back to check, I know, worried about all those cheap bedroom radios, the black-and-white telly portables, worn purses with their five-dollar bills and the savings books hidden beneath old underwear, the loose change, the small plastic boxes of junk beads and rings, the private tins of tea and cocoa and the little hot water jugs (no eating allowed in the rooms), the packets of cheating biscuits, the rare over-read letters and Christmas cards dated three years back now and the only real link with the outside world.

I have broken and entered.

I am an intruder. I have always been an intruder: on mother and aunt and father and husband.

I close my eyes against the implications of this and sit on assimilating those vibrations Mr. Lockyer might have felt. Once he also sat here, his chalky bones aching, catching glimpses of the too blue sea through the front door under the great washings of light, the garden greenery behind the stairwell window. My feet move gently back and forth, back and forth, in the foot pattern he made.

Time passes. I think I might have dozed. The thumping of the radio judders me awake from a distorted dream of Seb and I remember that three months before I left (how everything I encounter holds the spurious sheen of the present rather than the past!) he had taken to the radio with a hatchet. It was the national radio and the house had been shuddering for half an hour with whining pop music. "It sounds," screamed Seb, his nerves tattered (he had been trying to mend an electric kettle) and timing each word to a murderous thwack, "as if they're singing through their dicks. A horrible yellow stinking trickle!

"Trickle trickle trickle!" he roared, whacking.

I had waited until he flung radio remnants and hatchet out over the veranda railing.

"Well, that's positive," I said. "That's the most positive thing you've done in years. I approve. I wish I'd had the pleasure."

"I've chipped the table," Seb said apologetically. "Well, actually, I've smashed it."

"But only on one side. And it was only a small table."

Like
that
table
at
Villa Marina, 1973
or this table
beside my vinyl chair
in a strange boardinghouse at Tin River.

The parallels meeting, however far they are produced.

I look at my watch. It is past lunchtime. There is a small cough above me, a jerker meant to intrude and I see the old man standing righteously on the bottom step.

"Still here, eh," he comments. "What name did you say?"

I inspect his tired face which is deeply lined and leeched of color like a dried-out fruit. The mouth, however, quivers with an amusement that his eyes reflect.

"My name?"

"Any name. Yours will do." He grins for me and I like that.

"Of course. I'm sorry." I struggle to remember my married name and find it escapes me. My maiden name is gone. "Hunter?" I suggest.

"Hunter," he repeats after me. He utters the syllables again as if he is biting a coin to test it. I'm sprung! By now he would have been downtown and uncovered my car and motel identity. We stare at each other like failed guests at a party and in concurrence with my breakdown—I am sure it is a breakdown—I faintly hear Bonnie drumming away somewhere in the core of the building, tapping along to Aunt Marie's jazzed-up version of "The Rustle of Spring," played with swung quavers. And there's a trumpet as well.

"Listen!" I say to him. "Listen! Can you hear that?"

He lifts his head, cocks it sideways.

"What?"

"That music. Someone's playing somewhere."

"Can't hear a thing," he says, "except that damn radio. Mind, the hearing isn't what it used to be. You could be imagining things."

He is sure I am imagining things. He's dealing with an idiot, harmless, but someone to watch.

"No. It's not the radio. Listen."

Should I tell him I have a torn and life-sized depiction of a former resident of this place folded in my car trunk, crushed by the weight of that same resident's ancient chip heater? (Mr. Lockyer regrets he's unable to lunch today.)

My demeanor shuts the poor old devil up for by now I am throbbing with sound that doesn't reach him.

"I will be booking in here," I tell him. "Almost indefinitely. I have decided."

"You'll have to wait till the wife gets back," he says. "Be a while yet."

"Fine," I say. "That's just fine."

"Well, if that's all right then," he says suspiciously. "You want a cuppa or something?" I shake my head resolutely and I watch him lumber arthritically up the stairs, taking them ever so slowly, pausing on the landing to inspect me once more before trudging upwards.

I want to follow him.

I want to snoop in and out of every room on that upper floor. No. Not every room. Gaden's room. The last room along the front that opens onto the upstairs balcony.

I am holding his last journal.

Christmas, 1922, I read again. And again. He is using a fountain pen, clumsy ink droplets fading into a moving spatter. *Lost in my own port.* (I like that. Gaden, you were a poet as well as an embezzler. Embezzlement requires a flair for imagery, I excuse him.) *Everything about this place—the other inmates, prisoners, really, the food, the care or lack of it, seem sufficient punishment for any public error I might have made. My room is the most southern upstairs and I can walk from my bed each morning to the veranda and spend the day watching an indifferent sea.* (Indifferent? Ah, if only we had met earlier, later, whatever it required in the same time plane.) *I must forget the public nightmare and remember the good things. There's little time to remember, anyway. And who in the public sphere remembers me? It's all so brief. So brief. Here on this salty veranda watching the sea which has watched this shoreline, unchanging in its spitting comments for millennia.*

I'm blessed to discover my smallness.

I continue to sit, half dozing, half waking, as the day crawls slowly through midafternoon, presenting a negative of total innocence to any doubting passer-by. I have missed the sounds of lunch. My eyes are opened again to the yardman/husband scrubbed up for his late-afternoon stroll along Tin River's main street. He is wearing an open-necked shirt, too young for him, the sporty white trousers of a lawn bowler and sandals through which his broken toenails jut out.

"I'll be blowed!" he says, staring. "Still waiting! You must be stiff as a board."

I believe the state is known as catatonic. Am I? My caution is numb as well.

"I told you," I state emphatically, "I'm waiting for Mr. Lockyer." Madness becomes stubborn.

"I told you, lady, there's no one of that name here."

"There was. There certainly was. He has been booked in for many years. And in any case I wish for a room myself."

"No one called that in my time," he says, "and I've been here fifteen years. Think you must have got it wrong, somewhere. Wrong name or wrong address. And I can't give you any help about a room. The wife handles all of that. We're just about booked out," he lies.

Cobalt shadows reach in from the sea and lick along the skirting boards, creeping to the stair risers where the window blazes with western sun. My depletion is now so total I have barely the strength to marvel at my own persistence that keeps suggesting futilely that if I stay, if I can only endure, it might happen. I might break through. The rational side of me views the whole world now as one rocking ocean on which millions of lifebelts flaunt their white circles of security while I flounder among them unable to touch even the circumference of one of those rings, let alone insert myself into its saving center.

When I dozed through the long afternoon, the ancient dwellers of this house must have revived and strengthened, moving shadowily through upstairs rooms. I hear Gaden Lockyer's slippered feet shuffle along the corridor immediately above where I sit. I hear drawers pulled out, a cupboard slammed, the sound of taps being turned on and off.

Any moment, I tell myself. Any moment.

I ignore the old man in front of me. I deafen myself to whatever he is saying. I stare into and beyond him for by now he must be thinking of the police and the motel must already be making inquiries about my gate-crashing car.

He retreats a pace from my gummy fixed eye, scratches his head and says, "She'll be back soon, the missus. Any old tick of the clock." He's grunting and mumbling to himself, longing to turf me out but frightened of the dragon wife if he evicts a potential client. There can't be too many people busting to stay in Tin River.

I don't see you, old gardener. I don't see. I refuse to see. The corridor is changing before my eyes, walls moving back, melting, until the former dining and sitting rooms of the once retirement Tin River nursing home appear as they were, a piano angled across one corner of the parlor with a bowl of plastic daisies on top, recovering from its latest struggle with the rustling of spring. Somewhere a supper gong is clanging. How do all these old folk cope with the stairs? The yardman recedes through mists. I dress him in bowyangs and a sundowner hat and he vanishes as the beaten dinner gong explodes in brassy bursts like a stale sunflower through the hot oil fish stink of dinner.

Here they come—I can write about only what I see or think I see—stumblers limpers fragile old women delicate as pressed flowers men hobbling in crumpled trousers with their shirts open on wattle necks, skins blotched with years and sun cancer—all drawn to the sunflower, weary of time and not totting the paces of the sun, counting their own, painfully counting. How does the Blake go? How? *Seeking after that sweet golden clime* . . . it is the next line that is all-important . . . *where the traveller's journey is done*. Done. Finished. I recite the stanza aloud for the yardman, passing imperceptibly into a misquotation of Thomas More. Bollocks! I think. These trudgers are beyond worship or turning the adoring eye. They're counting the calvary of footsteps as their own sunflower drags itself towards Helios.

Ten of them I count, passing me without speaking, reflexed out of their lonely narrow cells all along the upper corridor and down the stairs, trailing after a blue-clad nurse who is jollying them along, while a matron masquerader together with the kitchen maid (May, Allie, whoever, timeless faces shifting from present to past to present, whichever it is as time refuses to move) wait at the ready beside the opened dining room door for us (I include me) to file past.

My head is an attic, a lumber room: packing cases, chipped furniture, the screwed-up tinsel and wrappings from lost feast days, musty letters, books, magazines and journals and everywhere cobwebs. I want to have this attic, this lumber room, whistled through, scoured by a sharp wind off any sea at all from the harbors in the islands, rid of the huggermugger fantasy of poetry or obsession or even that longing for the center, until there is nothing whiter than the gleaming inner walls of my skull.

My mouth keeps shaping *excuse-mes* to these passing ghosts.

Excuse me excuse me I am shouting in what does not even emerge as a whisper above the mad music-making of mother and aunt, my effort exhausting me so that I seem, but only seem, to sleep again as the last figure limps down the stairway, arrogantly late as befits a man who was once a public figure, and I am congealed in a cold and stiffening numbness and only wake—when is it?—hours weeks years earlier or later to a concerned hand light on my shoulder and a voice close by my ear.

I look up into a baffled smile that expands from world rim to world rim, the ultimate diameter, and find, above mine, eyes that are bewildered and ageless. The face is as familiar as my own but then my own is no longer familiar at all.

I have broken through, beyond the photographic ghost.

I have come to the other side of the picture and the lights in the early dusk outside are not those of a car but buggy lamps and the noises of the outer world are not the slamming of car doors but a snuffle of horses and the scraping measures of their hooves and the sea sound is drowning the notes beaten out by long lost mother father aunt and there is a fussing of hands that seem to be raising and supporting as I explore this puzzled smile.

The smile shapes itself into words and I gather each one like a shell.

"Are you waiting for me?" the lips ask.

July 20th. I have begun my own journal, paralleling, I suppose, the one that brought me to this place.

I have now been staying here in the boardinghouse at Tin River for over three weeks. Very soon my money will run out. I am becoming quite attached to the manager. She decided at once, that early evening three weeks ago, that I was harmless and needed looking after. Perhaps she could become my center. Even her husband/yardman is kind and brings me small posies from the garden. Perhaps they both could become my center. There is no other center here.

I am sitting in the most southern room on the upstairs veranda and it is empty of everything but me. Below in the roadway, my car is parked reflecting the sun. The trunk has been emptied of the chip heater which the old man freighted to mother a fortnight ago. That means it will reach her soon.

I am beginning to find my absorption *outside* me rather than *within*. Peripheral. This is hard to explain. Gaden Lockyer is returning to print rather than inhabiting my mind. I do feel I have been ill. I have sent off half a dozen postcards during the last week. On each of them I drew a perfect circle by inverting my breakfast teacup and tracing around the rim. At some distance outside the circle I put the smallest of points. The center lost outside its own